The Captain's voice startled the young lady at work in her garden.

"Why, yes," she said coming towards him. "It is Jane. Jane. Hampton. May I know why you ask, sir?"

"Forgive me, Miss Hampton," the young man said. "It is only that I have just returned from the Peninsula, and remembering English scenes like this was one of the things that helped keep me going. Thank you for making my homecoming so perfect."

"Pleased to be of service, Mr....?"

"Captain Edward Tremaine, at *your* service," he said, making a creditable bow.

Jane responded with a neat curtsy and friendly smile. "I am pleased to make your acquaintance, Captain Tremaine, and am glad you have returned home safely." She selected a half-opened deep pink rose from her basket and presented it to him.

Edward held it to his nose and inhaled its scent deeply, then stuck it through the buttonhole in his coat.

"Thank you a second time, Miss Hampton," he said, letting his gaze linger on the lovely lady in her English garden. "I hope we shall meet again."

"I hope so, Captain Tremaine," she said warmly. *I truly hope so.*

Books by Lucy Muir

HARLEQUIN REGENCY ROMANCE

18–THE IMPRUDENT WAGER

SUSSEX SUMMER

LUCY MUIR

Harlequin Books

TORONTO • NEW YORK • LONDON
AMSTERDAM • PARIS • SYDNEY • HAMBURG
STOCKHOLM • ATHENS • TOKYO • MILAN

Published September 1990

ISBN 0-373-31133-8

Printed in U.S.A.

CHAPTER ONE

CAPTAIN EDWARD TREMAINE drew his bay to a halt at the top of the rise and contemplated the view before him. The sun had burned away the morning clouds and its rays had since warmed the small village of Staplefield, nestled between the sliding green Sussex hills. Here and there the early summer verdant terrain was adorned with patches of pink and white where a late tree bloomed or flowers blossomed. Edward sighed contentedly and felt a sense of peace descend upon him—the first he had experienced in years. How often had dreams of such a rare June day in England sustained him, particularly this last year amidst the cold and barren mountains of Spain.

Memories of the retreat to Corunna threatened his new peace of mind, and he prodded his mount forward, eager to reach the security of his home and family. It was not far now. Two miles beyond the village and he would be home again. He had not seen Haverton Park since he had purchased his commission five years ago, although he had managed a visit or two to the family house in London.

The bay ambled forward at an exasperatingly slow gait. At this rate he would not arrive home for hours yet, he thought. He urged it to go faster, but it placidly ignored his direction.

"You know I barely have the strength to hold the reins, don't you, Ariel?" he said aloud.

Four months in hospital had kept him in the world of the living, but had done little to restore a body ravaged by dysentery and debilitated by starvation and exhaustion.

Edward resigned himself to the bay's slow pace. Just as well, he thought, since he had purposely arranged to give his family time to prepare for his return. He had sent his valet ahead with the carriage and luggage, both to give his family notice of his impending arrival and to enable him to drink in the country air and treasure every step of his homecoming.

As he slowly neared the village, a soft warm breeze carrying the heavy sweet scents of honeysuckle and roses ruffled the lock of blond hair falling across his forehead. He looked in the direction from which the breeze came and saw a pretty cottage covered in vines and brambles by the road not far ahead. It was a good-size cottage, built in the style typical of the region, constructed of brick and tile with wooden casements. What distinguished it from the others in the village was the profusion of blossoms covering both the cottage and the low stone wall surrounding it.

As he drew abreast of the cottage, Edward looked over the gate and pulled his horse's reins involuntarily, enchanted by the picture before him. A young woman clad in a pink print frock and straw hat knelt amidst a garden of early summer blossoms, a basket of cut flowers beside her. A fat marmalade cat sat in the middle of the garden path, twitching its tail as it stared at the stranger by the gate. The young lady, absorbed in her task, was not yet aware of his presence. Edward stared at her unabashedly, absorbing the perfect Englishness of the scene.

"Please," he said to the girl, almost unaware that he spoke aloud, "tell me your name is Anne, Susan or Jane."

The young lady started, knocking the basket of flowers sideways, and rose hastily to her feet, looking up at him in surprise. Her eyes reflected a temporary expression of shock, and Edward smiled ruefully as he realised the picture *he* must have presented, thin to the point of emaciation, his uniform hanging on him loosely. He half expected her to vanish into the cottage without a word, but instead she righted her basket and came forward to the gate.

"Yes, my name is Jane," she acknowledged in cultured accents, smiling at him, "Jane Hampton."

"I knew it had to be one of the three," Edward said. "The scene was so typically English that you had to have a good English name."

Her laughter was low and musical. "I am sorry to disillusion you, but if it's a good English name you seek, you should have asked if my name were Mildred, Audrey or perhaps Ethel. Jane is from the French, and Susan and Anne are of Hebrew derivation."

Edward laughed appreciatively. Now that he saw her close up, he realised that she was a little older than he had first thought, perhaps in her early twenties. She was of medium height and build and looked glowingly healthy with her pink cheeks and shining soft brown hair and eyes.

"My scholarship is shown up, isn't it, Miss Hampton? The derivation of your name aside, if you only knew how long I have yearned to see just such a scene."

He broke off, gesturing towards the cottage and garden. She smiled at him quizzically, and he endeavoured to explain his comment.

"I'm just back from the Peninsula, and remembering English scenes like this was one of the things that helped keep me going. Thank you for making my homecoming so perfect."

"Pleased to be of service, Mr....?"

"Captain Edward Tremaine, at *your* service," he said, making a creditable bow from his seat on Ariel, who was contentedly munching on the tall grass growing against the stone wall. Did he imagine it, or had a shadow darkened her eyes momentarily at the mention of his name? He decided he was mistaken, for she answered pleasantly enough.

"I am pleased to make your acquaintance, Captain Tremaine, and glad you have returned safely home," she said with a neat curtsy.

Edward knew he should be getting on, but was reluctant to do so. He said nothing for a moment, continuing to gaze about him, wishing to imprint the tableau upon his memory. Miss Hampton stood quietly, the breeze ruffling her skirts and carrying another wave of scent to his nostrils. The marmalade cat had evidently decided he was not worthy of notice and was busy washing its foot.

"May I have a rose, Miss Hampton?" he asked impulsively, wanting a memento.

"Of course." She went to her basket and knelt beside it, taking her time selecting one. She found one she felt suited the occasion and returned to the gate, holding it out to him. Her soft fingers touched his desiccated ones for a moment as he took the rose, a half-opened blossom of deep pink tinged with lavender, from her. He held it to his nose and inhaled its scent deeply, then stuck it through a buttonhole on his coat.

"Thank you, Miss Hampton," he said simply, smiling at her. She smiled back, a dimple appearing in her left cheek. Reluctantly Edward decided he must move on, and flicked the reins. However, Ariel, not having had his fill of the grass, took exception to this and turned back his head to glare at Edward, and then abruptly jerked his head forward and down, pulling the reins from his hands.

"It would seem Ariel has no more desire to leave your company than I." He laughed as he leaned forward to retrieve the reins.

"Ariel?" Miss Hampton laughed, "From *The Tempest*?"

Edward understood her surprise, for a horse which looked less like an airy spirit than the ponderous bay was hard to imagine.

"Yes. I chose him because I knew I couldn't handle a horse with spirit yet. I was feeling in an ironical mood when I named him, but I have found it to be more apt than I realised. He is a most capricious mount."

As though to verify his comments, Ariel suddenly decided to leave. He raised his head and started down the road at a brisk trot, only giving Edward time to wave a quick goodbye. His last view of Miss Hampton was of her leaning on the gate watching him disappear down the road towards the village.

JANE HAMPTON STOOD at the gate several minutes, gazing after her unexpected caller as he continued on his way through the village. So that was the elder son of Viscount Tremaine. She would never have guessed who he was from his appearance. He was so gaunt and haggard that she had missed the resemblance to the other members of his family but for the same hazel eyes and fair complexions. He must have been seriously injured in the action on the Peninsula, or been extremely ill. She felt compassion for him, and regret that he was a Tremaine. She had instinctively liked him, and under other circumstances would have liked to have become better acquainted.

Jane sighed and, turning from the gate, resumed filling her basket with flowers, musing on the events of the past few years. When she and her father and sister had moved to Staplefield four years ago, they had got to know the Tremaines quite well. Although they were not rich, Jane's father, a clergyman and grandson of a marquess, was socially acceptable to Viscount Tremaine and his wife. A close friendship had begun to develop between the two families. If only her sister had not caught the eye of Viscount Tremaine's younger son, Jamie, she thought, cutting angrily at a rose stem and stabbing her finger. Putting the wounded finger in her mouth, she chided herself for attacking the innocent roses. Jamie had been at fault, not the lovely blooms.

Two years ago, Jamie Tremaine, eighteen, and down from school for the holidays, had met her sister Fanny, then seventeen, and had become enamoured with her beauty. During the year he had been away, Fanny had changed from a skinny girl of no consequence to a slender young woman with beautiful silver-blond hair and dark brown eyes that seemed to glow against her fair skin. After a year, and against the better judgement of both families, who pressured them to wait until James was of age, they had become engaged.

Then last winter Fanny became ill with a terrible fever. For weeks she had lain between life and death, closer to the latter. Eventually she had recovered, but her beauty was gone. Her beautiful hair had fallen out, and when it started to grow back it was of a darker hue. Her luminous eyes dulled and her porcelain complexion turned yellowish and transparent. Jane would never forget the look on James Tremaine's face when he had seen his betrothed for the first time after she had begun to recover. Nor would she forget the pain on her sister's when James had visibly recoiled from her, blurting out right there and then that the betrothal was off.

To give James's family their due, Lord and Lady Tremaine had been shocked and dismayed by their son's behaviour. They were going to force their son to continue in the betrothal, but Mr. Hampton had intervened, requesting that they not do so. However, to keep gossip to a minimum and save face for both families, they decided not to make the broken engagement public until Fanny was fully recovered. So Fanny was still nominally Jamie's betrothed, although she had not seen him again since that day.

Jane decided she had enough roses, and went to cut some spicy-scented fraxinella for her father's study. She thought sadly of the deterioration of their friendship with the Tremaines. She and her father still spoke to Lord and Lady Tremaine at services Sundays, but it was awkward. Inevitably the situation had strained relations between the families, particularly when Fanny steadfastly refused to see any of the Tremaines. Fortunately the villagers assumed the Tremaines did not call at the Hamptons' cottage because of Fanny's delicate health, but as she improved there would be questions if Jane and her father could not persuade Fanny to relent.

Jane picked up her now-full basket and walked to the cottage door, followed by Thomas, the marmalade cat.

She wondered what Fanny's reaction to the visit by Captain Tremaine would be. She doubted Fanny would have missed seeing it, as she spent most of her day on the settee by the drawing room window watching what happened outside. Since Fanny would not receive the Tremaines, she could not receive other callers without causing comment, and the days passed slowly for her. Mrs. Fairchild, the vicar's wife, did come by occasionally to leave a glass of calf's-foot jelly, but Fanny had no other company.

Jane took her basket into the cottage kitchen. Mrs. Reid, a comfortable-looking village woman who came to work days, handed her a vase filled with water. Mrs. Reid's eldest son, Ned, served as the Hamptons' ostler, and her husband did any heavy work that was required around the cottage. Jane began to arrange the choicest blooms in the vase for her sister.

"You'd never guess who stopped by our gate just now," she said to Mrs. Reid.

"Captain Tremaine," Mrs. Reid said as she continued to prepare the Hamptons' noon meal without a pause, expertly rolling out the pastry for the meat pie.

"How did you know?" Jane asked, surprised.

"I saw him from the dining room window when I was laying the table. In that uniform it couldn't have been anyone else. I heard from Mrs. Wilson at Haverton Park that he was expected to be released from hospital soon."

"Was he wounded or ill?" Jane asked.

"Ill. He's been in hospital since January recovering from dysentery and exhaustion."

Jane said nothing, thinking the news exemplified how much they had lost touch with the Tremaines. They had not even known the elder son had been ill. She felt compassion for Lord and Lady Tremaine. She well knew what it was to worry about a seriously ill family member. A bell interrupted her thoughts.

"That'll be Miss Fanny, wanting to know where you are and all about the visitor at the gate," Mrs. Reid said, wiping her floury hands on her apron. "You'd best go and satisfy her curiosity."

"Yes, although I doubt she'll like the news," Jane said with a sigh. She finished arranging the flowers and put on her brightest smile as she went into the drawing room. Her sister lay curled up on the blue damask settee by the window, propped up by cushions so she could look outside. Although Fanny was mending slowly, she was still frail. Her face, framed by one of the caps she wore to conceal her short hair as it grew back, looked pinched and thin. At least, Jane thought, her colour was much improved and she was beginning to gain back some weight. The thin arms that lay on top of the blue-and-white counterpane were not quite so skeletal. Jane felt Fanny would improve faster if she would make an attempt to go outside, even just to sit in the garden, but Fanny had resisted all her attempts to get her out of the house. She suspected Fanny's reason for not wanting to leave the cottage was a reluctance to be seen by those who had known her as a beautiful girl. That was the hardest thing, Jane reflected—the change in Fanny's character from a mischievous young girl to a withdrawn shadow reluctant to stir from the cottage.

"Aren't these roses beautiful?" Jane asked as she placed the vase on a small mahogany table near the settee. "They are especially fine this year." But her sister was not interested in the roses.

"Who was that on the horse stopped by our gate?" she asked interestedly. "I couldn't tell from this distance."

Jane pulled a ladder-back chair forward and sat next to her sister.

"It was Captain Edward Tremaine," she said reluctantly, and watched Fanny's interested expression become cold and closed.

"He stopped to admire the flowers because he said imagining the English countryside had helped to keep him going when he was serving on the Peninsula," Jane continued. "He was so weak he could hardly handle his horse. Mrs. Reid told me he has been ill with dysentery."

There was still no comment from her sister. Jane leaned forward and took Fanny's hand, looking at her earnestly. "Fanny, can't you forgive what is past? All the Tremaines are not like Jamie."

The closed expression disappeared to be replaced by one of vulnerability. "Oh, Jane, I can't," she cried.

Jane sensed her weakening and pressed on. "You need not see Jamie yet, you know. But what of Lord and Lady Tremaine? People are going to begin to wonder why no one from Haverton Park calls, when you must be recovering by now. And think of Father—he misses his friendship with Lord Tremaine."

For a moment Fanny said nothing, her eyes staring bleakly at something beyond the far corner of the room. Then she spoke, her voice barely audible.

"I'm sorry, Jane, I just can't. I can't bear to see the pity in their eyes. I know people will think it odd the Tremaines don't call when I'm supposed to be betrothed to Jamie, but I just can't."

She paused, but Jane said nothing, afraid to break Fanny's confiding mood.

"I shall never forget the look on Jamie's face that day," Fanny continued, her voice faltering. "If I could be beautiful again—but I never shall be. I know it makes it difficult for you and Father, but please give me more time." She stopped and looked at Jane, her dark eyes pleading.

"Of course," Jane answered, patting Fanny's hand, "but you will not be able to avoid him forever."

"I know," Fanny said with a sigh, closing her eyes as if to shut out the world. She did not open them again, and in a moment her breathing became soft and regular as she fell into a light sleep. Thomas jumped up on the settee beside her and, turning around twice, joined Fanny in a nap.

Jane released Fanny's hand and went to the kitchen to arrange the remaining flowers, thinking that it would make things more than difficult if Fanny avoided the

Tremaines. The Tremaine family was a desirable addition to country society and they were accepted and invited everywhere. If the Hamptons were observed to be on unfriendly terms with the Tremaines, *they* would surely lose their acceptability, *not* the Tremaines. However, she really could not blame her sister for feeling as she did. She sighed, her love for her sister warring with her affection for the Tremaines and the knowledge that Fanny must someday face going back into the world. Perhaps Captain Tremaine would call again. Fanny might be brought to accept a member of the family who had not known her before her illness and could not make unflattering comparisons.

CHAPTER TWO

EDWARD'S FIRST VIEW of Haverton Park caused his heart to beat fast with anticipation. As he came through the trees and into the parkland that stretched before the house, the past six years were as though they had never been. Home at last! He surveyed Haverton Park with affection and pride as Ariel ambled towards it. The house had been built by the first viscount in the late fifteenth century. He had chosen Hugh May as his architect, a choice that proved to be felicitous. Mr. May had cleverly designed the house so that it appeared both homey and imposing, characteristics that might seem contradictory. Nevertheless, the warm stone and red brick with mullioned and transomed windows gave the house a cozy intimate look, while the imposing pilasters under the hipped roof gave it a stately air. Haverton Park was not the largest estate in the district, but Edward would not have traded his family home for any other.

As he rode up the neatly raked drive to the stone stairs in front of the house, the doors opened and several figures came out to stand before the steps. A groom ran to take Ariel, and as he dismounted, he was surrounded by family and servants and practically fell into the waiting arms of his mother.

"Thank God you are home safe at last," she said, holding him tightly. Then she released him and held him at arms' length, looking intently into his eyes as if she feared that should she look away, he would vanish.

Edward found his mother little changed, except that her chestnut hair, which proclaimed her Scots ancestry, contained a few more strands of gray. Her figure was still youthful, and her face unlined. Her clear hazel eyes glistened with suspicious moisture as they embraced once more before Edward turned to his father.

Viscount Tremaine was in his early fifties. His blond hair had darkened over the years, but his figure was still trim and muscular. He was more restrained in his welcome and did not embrace his son, but his hand gripped Edward's almost convulsively, and the emotion in his eyes could not be mistaken. Edward felt an obstruction in his throat, and turned to go into the house before his emotions got the better of him.

Dawkins, the butler, stood waiting to greet him on the steps, and Edward shook his hand warmly. He had been in the Tremaines' service as long as Edward could remember. The housekeeper, Mrs. Wilson, stood next to Dawkins, and Edward kissed her lined cheek affectionately.

The other member of his family who lived at Haverton Park waited to greet Edward in the large entrance hall. Edward remembered his younger brother as a gawky schoolboy of fifteen, and the foppish young man of twenty who stood before him bore little resemblance to that memory. He was evidently an aspiring dandy, for he was clad in the extreme styles which characterised that set. He wore a bright green coat, tight yellow pantaloons, a striped waistcoat and a perfectly creased and tied lavender neckcloth. His shining red-blond hair was carefully waved and arranged, and Edward could not tell whether the crimson cheeks owed their colour to rouge or chafing from the ridiculously high points of his shirt collar. The face was still boyish, but the frank schoolboy look had been replaced by an expression that managed to be both sulky and superior.

Sensing that his brother would not care to embrace, Edward held out his hand. James took it gingerly and, after a limp shake, allowed it to fall. He was staring with horrified fascination at something on Edward's coat, and looking down, Edward saw the rose he had placed there, now squashed and hanging drunkenly. He pulled it out of the buttonhole and addressed his brother, who appeared to be so shocked by the picture Edward presented that he was bereft of speech.

"Well, James, I see the schoolboy is gone and has been replaced by a man-about-town. It's good to see you again."

"Glad you're back safely," James said briefly. "Your valet's waiting in the front bedchamber," he added, sure that before anything else, Edward must desire the ministrations of that servant.

Edward smiled wryly at his brother and decided to take his advice. He promised to join his family in the drawing room shortly and went to have his valet remove some of the grime of his journey.

His old bedchamber was on the ground floor, just off the entrance hall, and Edward found it had been kept unchanged for him. Ames, his valet, had already put away his clothes and laid out fresh linen. He came forward to assist Edward out of his coat and then hesitated, looking at Edward's hand. Edward realised he still held the drooping rose. Reluctant to throw it away, he placed it between the pages of a book lying on the desk beneath the window. Wordlessly, he then placed himself under the expert care of Ames.

AN HOUR LATER, feeling much refreshed, Edward joined his family in the Green Drawing Room. He was grateful for the fire his mother had perceptively ordered to be lit, obviously sensing that in his condition he would chill easily. He leaned back against the smooth green damask upholstery of the Hepplewhite sofa and savoured the excellent brandy his father handed him. Smuggled no doubt, but he drank it without any feelings of guilt. He had served his country well.

"How's Mary?" he asked. Mary, his elder sister, lived in Yorkshire with her husband, Squire Deane, and their two children.

"She's doing well," Lady Tremaine replied. "She and George plan to make a visit here later this summer. You will enjoy little Tad and Lydia."

"Yes," Edward confirmed, "I am looking forward to seeing them." He could barely remember his nephew, and had never even seen his niece. It was good being part of the family again.

As Edward took another relaxing sip of brandy, his gaze travelled up to the ceiling where the graceful white plaster floral border caught his attention and admiration. It was a moment before he was aware of the uncomfortable silence which had descended upon the room. Recalling himself, he observed that his parents were regarding him with concern evident on their faces. James stood by the fireplace and studiously avoided looking at him at all. Edward couldn't blame them for their reaction to his appearance. The coat and breeches he had put on fit him no better than his uniform. A glance in the mirror in his bedchamber had told him that all Ames's skill had not disguised the fact that he looked little better than a walking skeleton. Edward took another swallow of brandy and broke the silence.

"Are you acquainted with the Jane Hampton who lives in the large cottage on the outskirts of Staplefield? The cottage with all the roses and honeysuckle?" he asked, to lighten the atmosphere and encourage a conversation. "I do not remember them living in the village before."

To his surprise, the question seemed to make his family more uncomfortable. His father cleared his throat noisily, and James appeared to be absorbed picking a speck off his coat sleeve. His mother answered, but her normally serene face appeared flustered as she spoke.

"Yes, we are acquainted with the Hamptons. John Hampton was the vicar of a parish near Bath. He came here about four years ago to complete a scholarly work he has been writing on Luke. His wife is deceased, but he has two daughters. Jane is the elder daughter, and there is a younger daughter, Fanny."

Edward opened his mouth to ask more about them, but before he could speak, Viscount Tremaine interrupted.

"Did you know there is a new Earl of Sedgworth?"

Edward's eyebrows rose in surprise at this sudden change of topic. He determined to question his mother about the Hamptons later. There was some mystery there.

"So Louis Grandville died," he said. "I'm sorry to hear that." Edward had always admired Lord Grandville, the local eccentric. Lord Grandville had felt that English culture had reached its zenith in 1773, and had refused to abandon his favourite year. He had continued to dress in the fashions in style that year, ate foods in vogue then and refused to purchase anything invented after that date. Once a year in August he had held a large masquerade at his estate, Bramleigh, to which he invited all the local gentry and aristocracy to show them the proper way an entertainment should be conducted, circa 1773, of course.

"Who inherited the title?" he asked.

"A great-nephew, Charles Grandville," Lord Tremaine answered, visibly relaxing as his son accepted the change of topic. "Odd thing was the way he left his estate. Although he could do nothing about the title, he provided that his heir would only receive the money and Bramleigh if he would continue his uncle's style of living whenever he would be in residence at Bramleigh."

James entered the conversation for the first time. "New earl's soft in the head if he don't contest the will. Look deuced silly in clothes more than two score and ten years out of fashion."

Edward looked at his brother consideringly. "They'd not look that much out of fashion. That's still the style required of one to wear at court."

"Court!" James scoffed at the thought of anything that fusty. He looked contentedly at his fashionable reflection in the glass above the fireplace and smoothed an invisible crease in his pantaloons.

Edward smiled. He couldn't like all the changes in his brother, but he supposed it was his age, although he didn't recall being like that himself at twenty.

"What's the new earl like?" he asked.

"Don't know," his father said. "He hasn't been in residence at Bramleigh yet, although his uncle died over a year ago. Perhaps he has been contesting the will, or perhaps he simply prefers to reside in Town."

The ice broken, Lord and Lady Tremaine brought Edward up-to-date on the rest of the gossip of Staplefield. Only the Hamptons were left out of the news, and Edward was more determined than ever to find out why.

EDWARD'S CHANCE TO ASK about the Hamptons came the next morning. Exhausted from his journey, he rose late and, after devouring a good-size breakfast, went to the small salon upstairs where he found his mother working on some embroidery.

Edward kissed his mother affectionately and sat across from her in a comfortable wing-back chair upholstered in blue-and-ivory brocade.

"Did you breakfast yet, Edward?" Lady Tremaine asked, laying her embroidery aside and looking at him with renewed concern.

"Yes. I had four rashers, three eggs, a kidney, some wheat loaf and two cups of coffee."

Lady Tremaine smiled at this complete catalogue of his meal and realised she was being overly solicitous. "Very well, I promise not to worry you about what you eat. Or anything else," she added.

Edward sat forward in his chair and spoke to his mother reassuringly. "Don't worry about me, Mother. Despite my frightful appearance, I assure you I am fine. I only need to put some weight back on."

Lady Tremaine nodded her acceptance of her son's diagnosis of his state of health, and Edward leaned back into his chair.

"Where's Father?"

"He's closeted with his new land agent, Benton, and Jamie is riding with Christopher."

"I gather from what was said last night that Jamie was sent down from Oxford last term. What prank did he pull?" Edward asked, remembering some of the jokes he and his friends had played on their masters.

"It was not a prank," Lady Tremaine said with a wry smile. "It was a matter of principle, or so Jamie maintains."

Edward waited for her to elaborate.

"He and Christopher Archer began wearing pantaloons mornings. They declared that breeches as morning wear were quite exploded, and they would not be caught in them before one o'clock. Unfortunately any students wearing pantaloons in chapel were marked absent. After several absences from chapel they were sent down."

Edward snorted, a sound between laughter and disgust. The story was of a piece with what he had seen of his brother since his return.

He remembered he wished to ask his mother about the Hamptons and decided to take advantage of their being alone and question her while there was little chance they would be interrupted.

"Mother, what is the mystery about the Hamptons? You all looked uncomfortable when I asked about them yesterday. Nor did you mention them when you were talking about the doings in Staplefield. Surely they are socially acceptable?"

Lady Tremaine folded her hands together in her lap and looked down at them a moment. Then she straightened her head with a sigh.

"I suppose I must tell you, although it does not reflect well upon Jamie. Of course the Hamptons are socially acceptable. We became well acquainted with them when they moved here and quite enjoyed their company. Mr. Hampton is a genial man, if a little abstracted, but that is to be expected in a scholar. His daughters are exceptionally nice young women. Fanny, the younger sister, was particularly beautiful. She and Jamie spent a great deal of time together, and last year they became betrothed."

"Betrothed? No one ever wrote to inform me of Jamie's betrothal!" Edward exclaimed, surprised at this piece of information. He also wondered why Fanny Hampton's beauty was spoken of in the past tense.

"The reason we didn't was that shortly after the betrothal, Fanny became quite seriously ill. We did not wish you to worry, so we did not tell you anything about it. Then..." Lady Tremaine faltered and looked past Edward through the window at the cloudless blue sky. Edward said nothing, and in a moment she resumed her story. "Then Jamie broke off the engagement."

"Why?"

His mother looked more uncomfortable than ever. "Fanny had been extraordinarily beautiful before her illness, but the fever destroyed her looks."

"And that is why he ended the betrothal?" Edward was appalled. Such behaviour was inexcusable in a gentleman and reflected poorly upon the whole family. "You and father allowed it?"

"Jamie did not consult us. When we heard what he had done we insisted he resume the betrothal, but Mr. Hampton was against it, quite understandably. We did agree that the engagement not be officially ended until Fanny was completely recovered, for the sake of both our families. Needless to say," she sighed, "our relationship with the Hamptons has become rather awkward. I tried to call upon Fanny once, but Jane told me she was not well enough to receive visitors. I gathered Fanny had refused to see me and did not call again. However, I suppose I shall have to make another call soon, or the gossips will begin to wonder why the family of Fanny's betrothed does not visit her in her convalescence."

Edward was silent several minutes. No wonder Miss Hampton had looked at him so strangely when he had introduced himself. It was a wonder she had remained to speak with him. How painful it must have been to her family to have the betrothal broken in such a manner on top of their other troubles. He must think of a way to rectify the situation. It certainly could not be allowed to remain as it was. Perhaps he could speak to Miss Hampton and persuade her to discuss with her sister the possibility of another call from his mother. She had been friendly enough to him.

"I spoke to Miss Hampton for several minutes on my way home yesterday. I had stopped to admire her flowers. Perhaps if I were to call upon her again I might be able to induce her to speak to her sister on your behalf."

Lady Tremaine considered a moment. "Perhaps that would be best. And as you are newly home from the war, Fanny might even be willing to see you. Despite her illness, she is a lovely child and will no doubt wish to welcome you home. And if she accepts a call from you, she will have to accept calls from the rest of the family, as well."

EDWARD INTENDED TO CALL upon the Hamptons the next day, but the journey home had taxed his strength more than he had realised. He felt too tired and weak to go anywhere for several days, and when he did feel recovered his father required his presence so that he might be brought up-to-date on the affairs of the estate.

It was not until a week later that he was able to set out of a morning for the Hamptons'. He had reluctantly ordered his recalcitrant bay to be saddled, realising that he could not yet handle his father's high-spirited cattle. Ariel might not mind his directions, but neither did he ever go faster than a trot.

He did not see Miss Hampton in the garden when he reached the cottage, so he tethered Ariel by the gate and walked through the fragrant garden to the cottage door. His knock was answered by a comfortable-looking woman of middle age who stepped back to allow him to enter.

"Captain Tremaine to call upon Miss Hampton," he explained.

"Please wait here, Captain Tremaine," she said. "I shall inform Miss Hampton you are here."

Edward looked around the small entrance hall as he waited. It was neatly but not expensively furnished, with Sheraton-style chairs and a bench. A small cherrywood clock ticked softly on a wall bracket, and a portrait of a young woman with two children hung on the wall. Edward was examining the portrait when a door at the far end of the hall opened and he was joined by Miss Hampton. She was clad in a blue muslin dress covered by a white smock, her unfashionably long hair piled atop her head and partially covered with a lace-trimmed muslin cap.

"Please forgive my appearance, Captain Tremaine," she said looking ruefully at her ink-stained hands and clothes. "I assist my father with his studies when he requires it, and I was not expecting company. Nor," she added confidentially, "does the plan of our house allow me to escape upstairs and make myself more presentable without you seeing me."

Edward laughed with her and assured her it was of no moment to him. Privately he thought her ink-smudged appearance quite charming, particularly when she smiled and her dimple appeared.

"I see where you acquired your scholarship, Miss Hampton," he said.

"Yes. I suppose Father has turned me into something of a bluestocking," she admitted. Edward thought if she were an example of a bluestocking, he had been missing something.

"I hope you are fully recovered from your journey?" Jane asked, the conventional question seeming to be spoken with evident sincerity upon her lips.

"Yes, I am feeling quite well, although my family finds it hard to believe when they look at me." He smiled engagingly, his hazel eyes warm.

Jane smiled back, feeling at ease with him despite being caught poorly dressed. She had wondered if he would call again after hearing about the connection between Fanny and Jamie. She was sure either Lord or Lady Tremaine would have told him of the betrothal. Evidently he did not consider it a reason not to further their acquaintance.

Jane realised she was being silent too long, but now that Captain Tremaine had called, she had no idea what to do with him. If she took him into the drawing room as manners demanded, she was not sure how Fanny would react. That was the trouble with living in a small cottage with only one drawing room, she thought regretfully.

Edward was beginning to wonder at her hesitancy when the door she had come through minutes before opened again, and a middle-aged man of slight build with silver hair and spectacles joined them.

"Captain Tremaine, may I present my father, John Hampton?" Jane said, feeling greatly relieved. If her father took Captain Tremaine in to meet Fanny, everyone would be more comfortable.

As the two men exchanged greetings, they took each other's measure, liking what they saw. Mr. Hampton opened the door into the drawing room.

"Please come and meet my other daughter and join me in a glass of claret," he invited. Edward went into the small drawing room, furnished like the entrance hall in Sheraton-style pieces.

At his first sight of Fanny Hampton, Edward was doubly ashamed for his brother. She lay on a settee by the window, the high-necked, long-sleeved frock she wore doing little to conceal her bone-thinness. Her head was covered by a large muslin cap, and enormous dark brown eyes looked at him warily from a pinched face.

"Captain Tremaine, this is my younger daughter, Fanny," Mr. Hampton said, as he tugged a bellpull to summon Mrs. Reid and order the claret.

"I am pleased to make your acquaintance," Fanny said courteously but coolly.

Edward took no notice of her thinly veiled hostility. He seated himself near her and smiled charmingly.

"It is I who am pleased to make your acquaintance, Miss Fanny. I am happy to see that you are feeling well enough to receive a visit from me. Finding that is so, I am charged by my mother to ask if you could sustain a visit from her next week. She is most eager to assure herself personally of your continued convalescence."

Fanny hesitated, her eyes going to her father's face. What she saw there moved her to answer civilly.

"Thank you, Captain Tremaine. Please tell Lady Tremaine I shall be very glad to see her next week."

Mr. Hampton gave Edward a glass of the claret Mrs. Reid brought in, and Fanny took the opportunity to study Captain Tremaine without being noticed. She had been reluctant to see a member of the family, but her face softened as she realised from his appearance that Captain Tremaine had also suffered from illness. She felt a bond between them, and when he turned back to her she no longer felt any hostility and conversed with him quite pleasantly.

After half an hour Edward rose to take his leave, not wanting to tire Fanny by staying too long. Mr. Hampton excused himself to return to his studies, and Jane accompanied Edward outside, walking with him to the gate.

Halfway down the garden path, Edward stopped and patted Thomas, who was sitting on a stone bench by the path, soaking up the warmth of the morning sun.

"Miss Hampton," he said, "may I speak to you frankly?"

Jane nodded, sensing what he wished to discuss.

"My mother has told me about the circumstances surrounding the betrothal between your sister and my brother. I am pleased your sister agreed to see my mother. She was concerned there might be undue speculation if Fanny continued to refuse to see the family of her supposed fiancé. The fiction of the betrothal need not be sustained much longer, but I think it better for your sister's sake that it be continued awhile yet. And even more for ours," he admitted candidly. "It would do our consequence no good if it were to become generally known how shabbily my brother has treated Miss Fanny."

Jane frowned at the remembrance. "I believe you are correct, Captain Tremaine. The betrothal should appear to die a natural death after Fanny recovers and rejoins society. I realise that in order for that to happen it is necessary that relations between our families resume their normal aspect." Her frown cleared and her naturally pleasant expression returned. "Besides, I have missed my association with Lady Tremaine, and I know my father has missed his friendship with Lord Tremaine."

"As they have you," Edward said, and repeated the conversation he had had with his mother. "We should like you to call at Haverton Park again, as well."

Jane hesitated. "Perhaps when my sister is a little stronger, but I cannot promise. You must understand Fanny's reluctance to see Jamie."

"I do, Miss Hampton," Edward assured her, "and I cannot tell you how much I deplore my brother's behaviour. But painful as it might be, your sister will have to face him some time in order to break off the engagement, which is all to her good. In the meantime, she should be encouraged to get out of doors more and take some exercise if she is to recover fully. I know that from my own experience."

Jane looked at him discerningly. He *was* looking better in just the week since she had last seen him. His hair was still dull and his civilian clothes were as loose as his uniform, but his colour was better and he had an air of generally improved health.

"Perhaps you could help me persuade Fanny, Captain Tremaine," Jane suggested. "I have tried to get her to go outside, but to no avail."

Edward stood up and walked to the gate. "Perhaps between the two of us we shall."

They exchanged a smile of complicity as Edward untethered Ariel, and Jane was very glad for the good fortune that had caused Captain Tremaine to stop and speak to her on his way to Haverton Park last week.

CHAPTER THREE

CAPTAIN TREMAINE CALLED upon the Hamptons the next three mornings, and Jane was pleased to see that Fanny accepted his visits and even looked forward to them. Jane found herself anticipating the visits even more than Fanny. She was careful not to be caught in her ink-stained smock again and began assisting her father in the afternoons instead of the mornings.

The visits from Captain Tremaine soon established a pattern. After he talked with Fanny in the drawing room for a half-hour, Jane would accompany him outside and he would sit another twenty minutes or so in her garden, talking of various things. His company was a delight to Jane, who was unaccustomed to having a male friend. He teased her gently, but always gave her opinions careful consideration.

The fourth morning after Captain Tremaine's initial call on Fanny, a carriage stopped at the Hamptons' cottage gates. Lady Tremaine alighted, but to Jane's disappointment, Captain Tremaine was not with her. Jane welcomed Lady Tremaine in the entrance hall, and Mr. Hampton emerged from his study to pay his respects. Lady Tremaine behaved with perfect cordiality, as though the only reason she had not called before was Fanny's poor health. Still, Jane followed Lady Tremaine into the drawing room with some trepidation. Fanny had accepted Captain Tremaine's presence, but would she accept Lady Tremaine's? Mr. Hampton did not go into the drawing room with them, but disappeared back into his study, a breach of manners to which Lady Tremaine, used to the scholar's ways, paid no attention.

Fanny was sitting up in a chair this day, her feet resting on a brocade stool, her hands lying listlessly in her lap. She was clad in a heavy dress of merino despite the warmth of the summer day, and a shawl was draped about her thin shoulders. As she escorted Lady Tremaine into the room, Jane saw apprehension in Fanny's expressive eyes and smiled reassuringly. Lady Tremaine went immediately to Fanny's side and kissed her cheek.

"I am so pleased you are feeling well enough to receive me," she said, seating herself upon a chair next to Fanny and taking Fanny's frail hand in her own. Her face showed no reaction to Fanny's changed appearance, and Fanny relaxed. "Society has been sadly flat without your presence and that of your father and sister," Lady Tremaine continued. "I am determined to remedy that soon."

Fanny replied in a somewhat restrained manner, but soon thawed under Lady Tremaine's determined warmth. Jane gave an inaudible sigh of relief and joined them, pulling another chair forward. Lady Tremaine chatted in a lively fashion, bringing Fanny up-to-date on the local gossip. Jane noted with satisfaction that Fanny was looking more animated than she had in a long time, and then her attention began to drift. She was wondering where Captain Tremaine was this morning when a sentence of Lady Tremaine's recaptured her attention.

"I have the most interesting news to impart," she said, pausing a moment so her announcement would have the proper effect. Jane and Fanny looked at her expectantly, and she continued, "The new Earl of Sedgeworth is in residence at Bramleigh."

Her tidings had the desired impact. Her two listeners were speechless for a moment, and then began questioning her eagerly.

"When did he arrive?"

"What is he like?"

"Will he be staying long?"

Lady Tremaine laughed, her hazel eyes sparkling, pleased with the effect of her news. "I'm afraid I can't satisfy your curiosity yet. I only know he is in residence. Jamie and Christopher brought the news. They were out riding yesterday afternoon when they saw a carriage with his crest go by."

Jane saw Fanny stiffen slightly at the mention of Jamie's name, but her interest in the new earl overcame her reluctance to refer to her betrothed.

"Did they actually see the new earl?" she asked.

"No," Lady Tremaine responded, "but it was indeed he. One of our footmen spoke to a servant from

Bramleigh who was in the village, and he was told that the earl plans to stay several months."

"Do you think the new earl will really follow his uncle's wishes as to his style of life at Bramleigh?" Jane asked.

"I suppose he must if he did not contest the will," Lady Tremaine replied.

"I should think more of him if he did not contest the will," Fanny said. "After all, it was the old earl's money. The least the new earl could do is obey his wishes."

"I shall be curious to meet him," Jane said, wondering what sort of man the eccentric Louis Grandville had chosen as his heir.

"We all are," agreed Lady Tremaine. "I have already informed Lord Tremaine that he must call upon our new neighbour as soon as possible. Unfortunately he insists upon waiting until the earl has a chance to get settled in. Provoking man!"

Jane and Fanny laughed with Lady Tremaine, and then Fanny looked speculatively at her sister. "Jane, do you suppose you could get Father to—"

"No," Jane interrupted. "Even if we could persuade him to leave his books, he is not vicar of this parish and would not feel right in making such a call."

"I suppose not," Fanny agreed reluctantly.

"Don't worry," Lady Tremaine said. "You will have a chance to meet him. I am planning to hold a dinner in the new earl's honour. You will come, of course."

Fanny's eyes dulled, and her animation vanished. "I do not think I am up to the rigours of a night out yet."

Lady Tremaine refused to accept this excuse. "Oh, I cannot have it for a week or so.... I doubt I shall be able to persuade Lord Tremaine to call upon him for several days. By then you will surely be strong enough. And if I am not mistaken I strongly suspect that a quiet dinner party would be more likely to encourage your recovery than discourage it. You see, my dear, to be in company is good for the soul."

Before Fanny had a chance to make another excuse, Lady Tremaine rose to leave, her silk skirts rustling about her. "I must leave now so I do not tire you overmuch. I cannot say how pleased I am to see you recovering so well, and I shall be a frequent visitor. I know how dull it is to be forced to lie idly halfway between well and ill."

Lady Tremaine adjusted her hat in the mirror, and then turned to Jane.

"I have thought of just the thing to liven your sister's convalescence," she exclaimed. "I have a copy of *Marmion* that I have finished. You must come this afternoon and collect it for Fanny. I know she will enjoy it excessively."

Lady Tremaine could easily send a servant with the book, but Jane saw that she was attempting to restore the previous informal relationship that had existed between the two families. She and Fanny had often walked to Haverton Park of an afternoon to visit Lady

Tremaine and share news of the latest fashions and gossip.

"Thank you, Lady Tremaine," she replied. "I shall be glad to visit later this afternoon." And perhaps, she thought, I shall also see Captain Tremaine, since he did not come to call here this morning.

MRS. REID HAD ASKED for the afternoon off, so Jane had first to assist with clearing up after their lunch before she could dress for the walk to Haverton Park. She wished to look her best, and thought a moment before choosing a white muslin gown trimmed in red ribands. She tied a wide-brimmed gypsy hat over her brown curls and looked at her reflection in the glass with satisfaction.

It was not an unpleasantly hot afternoon, and she walked easily, arriving at Haverton Park looking almost as fresh as when she had set out. Dawkins showed her into the Rose Drawing Room on the first floor and went to inform Lady Tremaine of her arrival.

Jane considered the Rose Drawing Room to be the most charming room in Haverton Park. Lady Tremaine had furnished it in her favourite Hepplewhite furniture upholstered in rose silk. The backs of the chairs and the settee were heart shaped, and heart-shaped garlands of flowers were printed upon the rose-and-white-striped paper on the walls. A cream, rose, and green carpet continued the colour scheme, and the windows, which commanded a view of the garden behind the house, were hung with draperies of heavy rose damask.

Jane was standing by the window admiring the magnificent pink and white peonies in the garden when Lady Tremaine entered the room.

"I am sorry it took me so long. I thought I had left the book on the desk in my sitting-room, but it finally came to light in the library," she explained.

Jane turned from the window and took the gold-embossed volume Lady Tremaine extended to her.

"Thank you, Lady Tremaine. I know Fanny will enjoy reading this. Her taste in literature is not in accord with my father's, and I fear she is quite bored with her long convalescence."

"We must organise some outings and other diversions," Lady Tremaine said, sitting on the sofa and motioning Jane to sit by her. "For my son as well as Fanny. Edward is looking better than when he first arrived, but I fear it will be a long time before he is himself again."

Lady Tremaine's smile vanished as she thought of her elder son's poor health, and she and Jane exchanged a look of mutual understanding as they thought of their respective relatives' illnesses.

A maid entered with a tea service, setting it on the round table next to the sofa. Lady Tremaine gracefully poured Jane a cup. "Sugar?" she asked, holding the tongs above the sugar urn.

"Please."

"Do you think Fanny *is* well enough to attend a dinner party next week?" Lady Tremaine asked as she handed Jane the delicate pink jasperware teacup.

"I think she is *well* enough," Jane answered cautiously.

"May I speak frankly?" Lady Tremaine asked, pouring herself a cup. "I realise it will be very uncomfortable for Fanny to face Jamie in a social setting for the first time since . . ." She trailed off. "It will be uncomfortable for us all," she finished. "But the sooner the situation is faced, the sooner it will be forgotten, both by Fanny herself and the rest of our small country society."

"I know you are correct, Lady Tremaine," Jane agreed, "but, if you will allow me an observation. It is not only Jamie that Fanny fears to meet in public but also friends who knew her when she had her former looks. With all due respect, Fanny is young. Indeed, I am five years older, and I think I should feel the same. But I shall undertake to see that she attend the dinner."

"Good," Lady Tremaine said, patting Jane's hand. "I do understand how she feels, but I think she will find she will not be the centre of attention she fears."

Their conversation was interrupted by the entrance of Captain Tremaine. Jane felt a slight tremor go through her body at the sight of him, and wondered at her response, for he was still too emaciated to be a handsome man. He was dressed in a blue coat, plain buff kerseymere breeches and a waistcoat of striped toilinette, none of which fit him properly. He smiled at Jane welcomingly, and her heart turned over.

"Good afternoon, Miss Hampton," he said. "Dawkins told me I would find you here with my mother. I hope your sister is feeling well today?"

As Jane thanked him for his concern and assured him of her sister's health, Edward looked at her with renewed admiration, enjoying the charming picture she made in her simple muslin frock and gypsy hat. Her robustly healthy good looks were very appealing to him after so many months of being in hospital with other ill people.

Lady Tremaine offered him some tea, but he declined.

"I wished to ask if I might accompany you on your way home, Miss Hampton," Edward explained. "I am on my way to Staplefield myself, to the tailor's, and I should be very glad of your company. Jamie tells me my appearance at the table quite puts him off his food, and much though it goes against me to agree with him about anything to do with dress, I must see his point," he said, looking down at himself with a comical expression of distaste.

Jane and Lady Tremaine laughed, and Jane gladly accepted his company. She finished her tea and, after thanking Lady Tremaine again for the book, left with Edward.

They began the walk to the village in a companionable silence, enjoying the peaceful sounds of the birds and the occasional breeze that rustled the leaves of the trees. Then Jane, unable to resist teasing him, asked, "Tell me, Captain Tremaine, why are you walking to the village? Is aught amiss with Ariel?"

Edward gave a shout of laughter. "I see you think I have been bested by my horse, Miss Hampton. But I assure you that is not the case. I walk because it is efficacious to do so."

Then his voice became serious. "Truly, Miss Hampton, every step I take I marvel anew that I am able to walk. There was a time I thought never to walk again. During the march to Corunna—" He broke off, looking apologetically at Jane.

Jane laid a hand upon his arm, looking sincerely into his eyes. "There is no need to hesitate to speak of your experiences to me, Captain Tremaine. I am a vicar's daughter, and know well the healing power of speech. Besides, I am interested."

Edward said nothing for a moment, thinking. It would be good to speak of his experiences in Spain to someone. So far he had told no one. He did not speak of them to his parents for fear of distressing them, and Jamie was bored by any conversation that did not centre upon dress. Besides, it simply wasn't done to speak of one's misfortunes. Would it do to unburden himself to the young daughter of a clergyman? He had become accustomed to discussing many subjects with Jane during his morning visits. Was this any different? He felt a surge of warmth toward Jane and took her hand, squeezing it in his. This must be what it was like to have a sister, to have someone truly concerned for your well-being.

"Thank you, Miss Hampton," he said, and, making his decision, began to talk slowly as they walked down the road, retaining her hand in his.

"Our problems on the Peninsula began before we even embarked for Spain. Castlereagh had directed that we be sent without equipment or food, trusting that we would find both once we got there. We were supposed to aid the Spanish in repulsing the French at Burgos, but by the time we arrived, the French already held Burgos, and the Spanish had lost their will to fight. Sir John Moore, our commander, had no choice but to take on the French army virtually unaided. Sir John knew that it would be wisest to leave Spain under the circumstances, but he also knew that the truth of the situation which he had encountered would never have been believed in England. He feared also that leaving would destroy what little remained of the Spanish morale."

Edward stopped speaking a moment, marshalling his thoughts in order to explain the remainder of the story to Jane in terms she could understand. Jane squeezed his hand encouragingly.

"So we stayed on. Sir John decided to divert the French by striking at Valladolid, drawing them away from Madrid and giving the Spanish an opportunity to regain lost ground. It worked—Napoleon came after us with his full strength, and Sir John, having drawn him successfully away from Madrid, began to retreat to Corunna, hoping to save the army.

"That was when things began to go wrong. Our only hope was to stay ahead of the French forces. They were much greater than our own, as well as better equipped and fed. But many of our officers did not see that. They resented not being allowed to stand and fight. We were so short of food that some of the men began to plunder the villages on the way. I never was more ashamed to be an Englishman! They—" Edward broke off, remembering to whom he spoke. There were things he could not tell her, vicar's daughter notwithstanding. His eyes looked bleak as he remembered how some of the men, wild with hunger and pain, had rolled huge casks of raw liquor onto the streets of a Spanish village, staving them with their bayonets and wallowing in the spirits as they ran down the streets. The atrocities which followed this undisciplined riot were unspeakable. With an effort he pulled himself back to the present.

"They were not all like that. The troops in the rear, those whom Sir John had trained himself, never lost their self-discipline and courage, no matter how hard they were pressed by the French. Convinced we would soon be destroyed, Napoleon left Soult to pursue us. We kept ahead of them by marching day and night through the snow-covered mountains. Many of our men died from exhaustion, and the rest of us were without shoes and stockings, our bleeding feet wrapped in rags, our bodies eaten with vermin. But we made it to Corunna, only to find—" and here Edward laughed bitterly "—that the troop transports were not there!"

He paused again, reliving the despair that had temporarily overwhelmed them all at the realisation that for all their courage, sacrifice and loyalty they would not get away before the French came upon them.

"By the time the transports arrived, the French had us surrounded, and we were forced to fight from a very bad position. But here at least the men redeemed themselves and fought so bravely that we held the French off and were finally able to embark. Unfortunately, without Sir John—he was killed the day before."

Jane had listened to Edward's recital carefully, filling in details where she could, realising that he had left out parts which he considered unfit for her ears.

"You thought a great deal of Sir John Moore, didn't you?" Jane asked gently.

"Yes. He was the finest man and greatest soldier I have ever known," he said simply.

They had reached the outskirts of the village now, and walked on in silence. As was proper, Edward dropped her hand, and the close companionship which had been symbolised by the connection was instantly missed by both of them. Passing the tailor's—which had been their original destination—Edward accompanied Jane to her cottage gate.

"Thank you for listening, Miss Hampton. You were right, a burden is easier to bear when it is shared, although I had little right to put it upon *you*."

"It is the least I could do, Captain Tremaine," Jane said, thinking of the burden those memories would be for him the rest of his life.

"Please call me Edward," he said impulsively. "And may I call you Jane?"

"Of course, Edward," she answered a little breathlessly, that strange tremor going through her again.

Edward smiled at her affectionately before leaving to walk back to the tailor's. Befriending someone such as Jane seemed to justify all the suffering of the campaign. It was for those such as her that they had fought the menace of Bonaparte.

Jane went into the cottage with a musing half smile on her lips. Her instinctive liking for Captain Tremaine was fast blossoming into something stronger, and now she felt she had evidence he felt the same. Surely he did, or he would not have asked leave to call her Jane and smiled at her in such a way. Bemused, she went into the drawing room to give Fanny the book from Lady Tremaine.

"Was that Captain Tremaine who walked with you to the gate?" Fanny asked after thanking Jane for collecting the book.

"Yes. He offered to accompany me home since he was on the way to the tailor's."

"Jane, you are not developing a *tendre* for Captain Tremaine, are you?" Fanny questioned. "You have only known him this past fortnight."

"Don't be ridiculous, Fanny," Jane denied, but she felt her cheeks flush and bent to hide them, ostensibly to pet Thomas, who rubbed against her skirts, demanding attention.

Fanny did not look at the new book in her hand for several minutes, thinking instead about Jane's suddenly pink cheeks and what they could mean.

CHAPTER FOUR

IT WAS NOT MANY DAYS later when Fanny sought Jane out in the kitchen where she and Mrs. Reid were discussing what purchases to make for the week.

"Lady Tremaine must have persuaded Lord Tremaine to call upon the new earl," Fanny informed them, looking at a card in her hand. "We have received an invitation to dinner Friday."

"Did a servant bring it?" asked Mrs. Reid, fearing she had been remiss in her duties.

"I was sitting outside in the garden when the footman brought the invitation, so I took it," Fanny explained.

Jane thought that Fanny going outside without encouragement was a good sign. Her attitude had improved greatly since the visits from Edward and Lady Tremaine, and her health had improved correspondingly.

"Lady Tremaine says they will send a carriage for us at half-past five," Fanny continued.

"That was thoughtful," Jane commented. The Hamptons' gig would not seat three comfortably and its ride was rough. The carriage ride would be much easier on Fanny.

Fanny walked slowly up and down the room and then stopped before Jane and Mrs. Reid.

"I know I cannot escape attending the dinner, but I wish I might. Or that Jamie would not be there," she burst out.

"If you wish your betrothal to appear to die a natural death, you must face Jamie soon," Jane said. "And the sooner you face it the sooner it will be over."

"Miss Hampton is right," Mrs. Reid agreed. "And we all have your best interests at heart. I have no doubt that once this business is settled you will make a more complete recovery."

"Besides, if being the centre of attention is your concern, I collect that everyone's interest will be upon the new earl at the dinner," Jane said soothingly. "I make no doubt Lady Tremaine planned it that way."

"I am sure you are right," Fanny said, "but that doesn't make it any easier." She went over to the window and looked at her dim reflection in the glass. A waiflike figure with huge eyes looked back. "How I wish I did not have to face him appearing as I do," she said forlornly.

Jane had no doubt who the "him" referred to was, and her heart ached to see her formerly high-spirited sister so cast down. She turned from her list making and tried to view Fanny dispassionately. She was still too thin, but her skin had regained its healthy colour, and her eyes looked large and luminous. Jane felt she would look quite unexceptional properly gowned, even pretty, but that was small solace to a young girl who had been an undoubted Beauty.

"Do you still have that blue silk, Miss Fanny?" Mrs. Reid asked abruptly.

Surprised, Fanny turned away from her reflection in the glass. "Yes, it is in my wardrobe."

Mrs. Reid pushed her chair away from the table and stood up. "Come upstairs and try it on. You come, too, Miss Hampton."

Mystified, Jane and Fanny followed Mrs. Reid upstairs to Fanny's bedchamber. Mrs. Reid took the gown out of the wardrobe and looked at it with satisfaction. It consisted of a white silk underdress with an ice-blue silk overdress trimmed in silver. She helped Fanny into it and stood a moment surveying her critically. The gown hung on Fanny loosely, making her look like a child dressed in her mother's clothes, but Mrs. Reid seemed undeterred. She took a packet of pins from her housewife and began pinning the gown to fit.

Jane sat on a stool at the foot of Fanny's bed, watching interestedly. In a few minutes she realised what Mrs. Reid had envisioned. If Fanny's frail appearance were *emphasised* instead of disguised, her looks were greatly enhanced. The ice-blue colour against Fanny's translucent skin gave her an almost ethereal appearance. She looked quite beautiful, if not in the same style as before.

Mrs. Reid finished her pinning and stood back to look at the results with satisfaction.

"If you would help me, Miss Hampton, we could alter the gown to fit by Friday. We have four days."

"You should have been a modiste," Jane said admiringly. "Look in the glass, Fanny."

Fanny slowly went to view herself in the gilt-framed mirror, hopeful, yet fearing what she would see. For a moment her face lit, but then she noticed what Jane and Mrs. Reid had forgotten.

"But my hair," she wailed. She pulled off her cap and stood dejectedly with her short wispy mouse-coloured hair flat against her head. It quite destroyed the fairylike appearance she had presented moments before.

Jane stood up and went to Fanny, fingering the short hair thoughtfully. Although it was of a silky fine texture, she understood why Fanny felt it was far inferior to the long silver-blond hair she had had before her illness.

"It is still short, my dear, but I think it's long enough to curl," Jane said reflectively. "We cannot do anything about the colour, but if I were to make a garland of roses to place in it, I think your hair will look acceptable."

"The very thing," Mrs. Reid agreed. "Don't you worry, Miss Fanny. We'll have you look a treat for the dinner."

Fanny shook her head doubtfully at her reflection, but obediently stood still as Jane and Mrs. Reid finished pinning and measuring for the alterations. She could not believe anything they might do would truly make her look acceptable.

THE DAY BEFORE his mother's dinner, Edward determined to speak to James about the situation with Fanny. He had not dared to do so yet, afraid that he would not be able to hold on to his temper. As he had got to know Fanny, he deplored his brother's shabby treatment of her more than ever. He could not imagine deserting such a fine young girl simply because a fever had temporarily robbed her of her beauty. His parents had been much too lenient on his brother, he felt.

As he expected, he found Jamie in his dressing room, absorbed in his reflection in the glass. Edward entered without knocking.

"James, I wish to speak to you," he said sternly.

"Can't it wait? I'm not finished dressing," Jamie said, frowning into the mirror with intense concentration as he tied his cerulean blue neckcloth. His valet stood nearby with two more carefully pressed ones ready in case Jamie were to make a mistake tying the first.

"No, it can't wait, and what I have to say would be better said privately," Edward insisted.

"Very well," James agreed sulkily, continuing to tie the neckcloth. "You may go, Blake."

"What is it?" he enquired as the valet went into Jamie's bedchamber, closing the connecting door behind him.

"It is about Miss Fanny Hampton," Edward replied, going to stand before the mirror and looking grimly into Jamie's face. Jamie apparently had no intention of facing his brother unless he were forced to.

Jamie looked sulkier. "Wondered if you'd been told. You needn't prose at me about it. Father already did."

"I'm pleased to hear it. Nevertheless, I'm also warning you. You had better remember that as far as our neighbours are concerned, you are still betrothed to Miss Fanny. I expect you to behave as though you are."

"I shall," Jamie muttered grumpily, sidestepping Edward so he could see his reflection in the glass. He gave the neckcloth a final crease. "Although what people will think when they see me playing up to such a fright I don't know," he said in an aggrieved tone. "I don't like it above half."

Edward's temper got the better of him at this churlish remark, and he took hold of Jamie by his freshly tied cravat, pulling it tightly about his neck.

"How can you have such a callous attitude toward a girl you supposedly loved? Or was it only her beauty you cared for?" Edward demanded. "You needn't reply—the answer is obvious. But if you do not dance attendance upon her tomorrow night, you will answer to me."

Edward gave the neckcloth a final twist and let go. Jamie rubbed his neck and breathed deeply.

"I say, no reason to get violent. You've ruined my cravat. I had it tied in a perfect Oriental. I'll have to start over,'' he said, carefully putting distance between himself and his brother. He reached the door to his bedchamber and opened it.

"Don't worry, I'll do the pretty,'' he called as he jumped through the door and slammed it behind him.

Edward looked at the door with disgust and left the room, shaking his head. What a coxcomb Jamie was turning out to be.

FRIDAY WAS UPON THE HAMPTONS before they knew it. Jane and Mrs. Reid had worked steadily on the gown for Fanny, and their work was rewarded that evening when they viewed the final results. Jane had embroidered a band of white roses around the hem of the ice-blue overdress and tied the long sleeves with new white silk ribands. A garland of white roses lay in the soft curls Mrs. Reid had coaxed into Fanny's hair, and she wore white satin slippers and carried a blue-and-white fan trimmed in silver. It was true Fanny did not have the spectacular beauty she had had before, but Jane felt the almost fairylike picture she presented now was far from a beauty to dismiss.

Mrs. Reid adjusted one of the ribands on Fanny's gown and then turned her attention to Jane. In her concern over her sister, Jane had not expended much time and effort on her own appearance. She wore a simple frock with a square décolletage and short sleeves in her favourite pink. She had completed her toilette with long silk gloves, a white sarcenet stole and a single pink rose in her hair. Mrs. Reid nodded approvingly.

"You are both in excellent looks," she proclaimed. "Don't worry about this evening, Miss Fanny. It will go well."

Jane seconded her pronouncement, and Fanny smiled bravely.

Mr. Hampton appeared from his study to wait with them for the carriage from Haverton Park to arrive. He looked unexceptional in a dark blue evening coat, breeches of cream-coloured nankin and a simply tied cravat.

"You look beautiful, my dears," he said to compliment them both.

Jane and Fanny exchanged looks even as they thanked him prettily. Their father would say they looked beautiful if they appeared in sackcloth and ashes. But the compliment served its purpose, and they went to climb into the Tremaines' comfortable carriage with bolstered confidence.

WHEN THE HAMPTONS were shown into the Green Drawing Room at Haverton Park, they discovered they were the first to arrive. Jane suspected her hostess had sent the carriage early so Fanny would see Jamie for the first time with no onlookers from outside the family. Viscount Tremaine, dressed like Mr. Hampton in a blue coat and cream breeches, welcomed them warmly and drew Mr. Hampton aside for a talk. Lady Tremaine, attractive in a high-waisted gown of green-and-yellow-striped lutestring, bade the sisters sit on a green brocade sofa and sat across from them on a square-backed chair. She complimented them on their looks, and her obvious sincerity seemed to remove some of Fanny's nervousness.

"Edward and James will join us shortly," Lady Tremaine said as Fanny glanced about the room, obviously looking for them.

Even as she spoke, the brothers entered the room, and Jane felt Fanny tense beside her. While Edward and James paid their respects to Mr. Hampton, Jane regarded them critically. Edward was looking much better in one of the new suits made to fit his slim figure, but the tailoring was obviously country—a coat, waistcoat and breeches all of plain olive green. Jamie, in contrast, was complete to a shade in a bright yellow coat, skin-tight blue nankin pantaloons, a red neckcloth, and striped waistcoat. As he and Edward came to greet Jane and Fanny, Jane noticed that Jamie looked quite ill at ease. As well he might, thought Jane indignantly.

"Good evening, Miss Hampton, Miss Fanny," Edward said easily. "You both look charmingly."

As Jane and Fanny responded to Edward's greeting, Jane saw Jamie start when he finally directed his gaze at Fanny. Jane could tell by his expression that he was surprised to see Fanny looking so well, and she felt easier for Fanny.

"Good evening, Miss Hampton, Miss Fanny," he muttered, repeating his brother's words. "Must say you're looking well. Pleased to see you at Haverton Park again, Fan."

"Thank you," Fanny said briefly, a trace of irony in her voice evident to Jane's ear.

The other guests began to arrive, and Fanny was spared a long conversation with Jamie. Baron Archer and his family were the first. Lady Archer was a handsome woman of middle age who was a close friend of Lady Tremaine's. Her son, Christopher, was of the same age as Jamie, and they also were close friends. Marianne, their daughter, was a shy girl of seventeen, not yet out.

They all expressed their pleasure at seeing Fanny back in society, and Fanny forgot her apprehensions. Marianne, who had always admired the older girl, sat by her side. Fanny's changed appearance had evidently not caused her to go down in Marianne's esteem. Christopher, too, stayed near Fanny and engaged her in conversation. Fanny lost the hunted expression she had had when she first entered the drawing room and began to relax.

The vicar of the parish, Mr. Fairchild, and his wife arrived soon after the Archers, along with Squire Shirley and his lady. The children of these couples were too young to attend a dinner, and had been left at home. The Archers and Shirleys also expressed their pleasure at seeing Fanny in society again, but Fanny was not the centre of curiosity and speculation she had feared. All were waiting expectantly for the arrival of the new earl, curious to see what their new neighbour was like.

"Charles Grandville, the Earl of Sedgworth," Dawkins finally announced with a flourish.

Everyone looked to the door of the drawing room and conversation ceased. The new earl paused a moment at the door before advancing into the room. Jane sensed he knew of the curiosity surrounding him and was purposely making a slightly late entrance.

He was much younger than Jane had expected, appearing to be only a little older than she, perhaps about four-and-twenty. He was evidently fulfilling the terms of his great-uncle's will, for he was clad in the fashion of the year 1773. He wore a semiformal suit of corded red silk with deep velvet cuffs, a powdered wig tied in the back with a black silk riband, high-heeled shoes with elaborate silver buckles and striped silk stockings.

Jane wondered a moment why the earl looked so odd in his old-style clothes. It was not at all unusual to see older men who preferred the styles of their youth. That was it, she realised, it was his youth. One never saw a *young* man in the older styles, except at court, and then only in the very formal full evening dress.

When it came turn for Jane and Fanny to be introduced, Jane thought she saw a spark of mischief in the earl's black eyes as he bowed over her hand and kissed it. She felt he fully enjoyed his new role as eccentric and was playing it to the hilt. He next turned to Fanny, and Jane saw the mischief in his eyes turn to admiration.

Instead of kissing the back of Fanny's hand, he gracefully raised her fingers to his lips and then extended his other arm down in an arc toward Fanny in an inexpressibly beautiful gesture. Fanny blushed and lowered her eyes, and Jane caught Jamie watching. He was very clearly looking at Fanny with new respect and a little jealousy.

Dinner was announced and the guests went through the double doors into the handsome dining room adjoining the drawing room. The late sun, softened by ivory draperies, came through the tall windows and warmed the pale blue room. The chairs surrounding a beautiful mahogany table were designed to look like shields carved with the stylised feathers that were so recognisable as a symbol of the Prince of Wales's Crest. A matching sideboard stood against the wall.

Jane was pleased to be escorted in by Captain Tremaine, and she was seated between him and Chris Archer. Fanny sat across from Jane, between Lord Grandville and Jamie. When they were all seated, the vicar was asked to say grace, and Jane began enjoying a delicious Madeira-flavoured mushroom soup.

Conversation became general and, as sometimes happened at informal country parties, was not confined to the persons on either side of the diner, but went across and around the table. Perhaps because of the number of gentlemen present, the conversation began to centre on the conflict on the Continent. Usually such subjects were left for after dinner when the gentlemen remained behind to enjoy their port and cigars. Baron Archer, a heavyset man of Viscount Tremaine's age, began praising Wellesley, the young lieutenant-general who was beginning to make a name for himself on the Continent. Suddenly he addressed Edward.

"Too bad you didn't have the opportunity to serve under Wellesley instead of Moore. Why, the reports coming back on Moore are quite shocking. It appears he wouldn't even let his troops stand and fight, but forced them to flee the French in disgrace." He shook his grey head in amazement and disgust.

Jane felt Edward stiffen beside her. After he'd told her of his experiences on the Peninsula, she knew how much the baron's comment must have upset him, but he was bound by good manners not to disagree too strenuously with a guest in his father's house.

"Read just the other day that he made a shambles of the whole campaign by not being able to control his troops," Squire Shirley added. "Would have defeated Bonaparte already if it hadn't been for his bungling."

Jane saw Edward's hand clench in his lap and impulsively placed hers over it. She felt his hand relax and he squeezed hers lightly.

Fortunately Edward was saved the necessity of an immediate reply by Lord Grandville. The earl was seated directly across from Edward and had apparently noticed his agitation.

"I believe it is a common enough failing for one to blame another for one's own mistakes. Sir John makes a good scapegoat since he is no longer here to defend himself,'' he said diplomatically.

The earl's comment helped Edward master his emotions and answer politely but firmly.

"Yes. I agree, Lord Grandville. In my experiences serving under Sir John, he always made the best decisions possible under the conditions. I hold his memory in the greatest respect."

The squire and Lord Archer looked doubtful, but to press the subject when they saw Edward was prepared to defend his former commander would have been in bad taste, and they said no more.

Viscount Tremaine changed the subject, and Jane, realising her hand was still in Edward's, withdrew it and helped herself to the dish of rabbit which Christopher had passed to her. She then placed it before Edward and he took some with a grateful smile. Conversation returned to more congenial subjects, and the rest of the dinner passed without incident.

Jane kept an eye on Fanny to see how she was coping with her first night back into society, and was amused to see that the attention Fanny was receiving from the earl was causing Jamie to become competitive. Seeing the woman he had rejected admired by others evidently made him wonder if he had been precipitate in ending the betrothal. He quite exerted himself to be charming. Fanny responded graciously, since the other guests presumed she and Jamie were still betrothed, but Jane was relieved to see that Fanny was cautious. She would not want her sister to become enamoured of Jamie again.

After the fruit was served, Lady Tremaine rose and the women retired to the drawing room. Young Marianne Archer attached herself to Fanny, and Jane talked quietly to the vicar's wife, Elizabeth, about parish matters. She noticed, however, that Fanny was beginning to tire, and soon after they were rejoined by the men she signalled to her father. They made their excuses to Lady Tremaine and left early.

Fanny relaxed into the soft squabs of the Tremaines' carriage on the drive back and sighed. "It was not as difficult as I feared it would be," she said.

"Things rarely are," her father replied mildly. He had been concerned about his younger daughter, but saw now that she would be fine. He could go back to his books without undue distress.

"The new earl quite singled you out for attention," Jane added. "I was surprised to see how young he is. He doesn't seem to object to the terms of the will at all. I wonder if he will continue the custom of the August masquerade?"

"I predict that he will," Fanny said. "I thought he looked quite elegant in his clothing. More so than some dressed in modish styles."

Jane looked sharply at Fanny. The earl had evidently made an impression on her, too. She hoped Fanny would not lose her heart again too soon, although it was good to note that she was not pining after Jamie.

THE DAY AFTER THE DINNER Jane knew that they were going to be welcomed back into society with open arms. Lady Archer and Marianne called in the morning, as did Mrs. Fairchild and Edward. Edward did not stay long, and Jane could see he was preoccupied. She wished she could talk to him, but the presence of the others prevented it. She could not leave her other guests to accompany Edward outside when he left, as had become their custom.

The afternoon brought several more callers, including Jamie and Christopher. While the two dandies were there, a basket of fruit and a brace of hares arrived for Fanny from Bramleigh. As Jane and Fanny exclaimed over the beautiful glass-house fruits, Jamie looked at Fanny suspiciously.

"It's only a basket of fruit," he muttered ungraciously.

After Chris and Jamie left, Jane teased Fanny. "You were worried about nothing. Your beauty can't have changed that much when you already have three suitors the first day after you venture back into society. Jamie looked quite put out by the arrival of Chris and even more so by the basket from the earl."

Fanny smiled. "I begin to wonder what I ever saw in Jamie. He acts like a petulant child."

Jane was pleased to see the dramatic difference already evident in Fanny's attitude since the dinner the night before. She was not quite back to herself, but Jane now had confidence she soon would be.

In her pleasure over Fanny, however, she was still concerned about Edward. It had been very evident that morning that something was on his mind. The next morning Jane went to work in her garden early in the event that he came again, hoping she would be able to speak to him there.

Her hopes were realised. Not long after she began weeding the alyssum, Edward arrived. As he tied Ariel by the gate he spied Jane amongst the flowers and went to join her, sitting on the stone bench. Jane abandoned her weeding and sat beside him.

"What is it that's bothering you, Edward?" she asked.

Edward smiled ruefully. "I know I shouldn't burden you with my problems again, but somehow it is so easy to talk to you that I find myself tempted to do so."

"Please do."

"It's what Lord Archer and Squire Shirley said about Sir John Moore at the dinner. Yesterday I made a point of reading some recent newspapers through, and I am sad to confirm that there are terrible things being said of Sir John."

He stopped a moment and ran his fingers through his blond hair.

"I feel so helpless. They are spreading scurrilous lies, ruining his reputation and affecting how he will be remembered by posterity. I allow that Sir John was never one to tolerate incompetent politicians, and he used to put quite pointed remarks in the dispatches he sent back to London. Now I fear he must have made some very powerful enemies."

Jane sensed how very upset he was and thought for a moment. "Edward, is there no one you could see to clear his reputation? Someone in London who has influence?"

Edward brightened. "Of course. I should have thought. Perhaps one of my superior officers would know what I could do."

His forehead creased as he tried to remember if any of his former commanding officers who might have the influence to help him in his efforts were in London.

"I believe Colonel Wentworth is in London," he said thoughtfully. "He has some influence in political circles, as I recall. If he cannot do anything himself, I am sure he would be able to arrange meetings for me with someone who could."

Jane smiled at him encouragingly. "You see, there is some hope yet. I am sure you will be able to clear Sir John's name."

Edward did not reply to her optimistic statement, seeming hardly aware of her existence as he stared off into the distance, planning the journey before him.

"I must arrange to leave immediately," he mused, more to himself than to Jane.

Jane regarded him with reservation. Although there was no doubt his health was greatly improved, he was still thin, and she had observed that he tired easily.

"Are you sure you are feeling well enough to make the journey at once? Perhaps you should wait until you have recovered more of your strength,'' she ventured to advise.

Her words recalled Edward to Jane's presence, and he looked at her with an affectionate smile. Jane felt her heart quicken, for the tenderness evident in his expression was unmistakable.

''Thank you for your concern, but I feel sure I am able to travel if I go by carriage and take the journey in easy stages,'' he assured her. He stood up, eager to go now that he had a plan of action.

''What would I do without your wise counsel?'' he asked, and bent down, kissing her lightly upon the forehead. ''Please excuse me if I go without paying my respects to your father and sister. I must organise my journey and be on my way as soon as possible. I shall come to see you the moment I return.''

Jane walked to the gate with Edward as he took his leave, and then returned to the garden bench. She sat there a long time, feeling strangely bereft. A moment ago her heart had been full, now it was empty. What had she done, sending Edward away from her? A feeling of foreboding enveloped her. She tried to shake it off. It was nonsense; she was just feeling lonely at the thought of not having his company for a fortnight or so. What could possibly happen in a short trip to London?

CHAPTER FIVE

THE COUPLES on the dance floor made their final bow as the strains of the boulanger faded into the London night. Edward knew he should leave his half-hidden position by the windows and solicit the hand of one of the young ladies for the next dance, but he was reluctant to enjoy the gaiety. His health was much improved, but he still lacked the stamina to dance for long without it tiring him. He wished he might return to his hotel, but after Colonel Wentworth's kindness in assisting him in his efforts to clear Sir John Moore's name, he could not leave Mrs. Wentworth's ball so early.

A frown marred Edward's expression as he thought of his futile attempts on Sir John's behalf. Colonel Wentworth had obtained audiences for him with Canning and Castlereagh, but his appeals to them had been to no avail. Castlereagh, the war secretary, had listened politely but had been unhelpful, and as for Canning! Edward had thought, since Castlereagh and Canning, the war minister, were rivals, that Canning would assist him if Castlereagh would not. But Canning seemed to have an actual hatred for Moore. Remembering Sir John's impatience with inept politicians, Edward imagined that some of the pointed comments in the dispatches sent to London had been directed at the war minister. It would seem Grandville was correct—Sir John had been made a scapegoat for errors of politicians safe at home in London. His frown deepened as he thought of the wrongful blame foisted on as fine a man as his former commander had been.

"You're looking blue-devilled, Tremaine. Can't have that. Let me introduce you to a partner for the next dance."

Edward erased his frown and turned to his host with a pleasant smile. Colonel Wentworth was in the Household Cavalry, and presented a fine figure in his blue-trimmed red coat, grey trousers and shining black boots.

"Forgive me, Colonel. Thinking of my problems with the matter of Sir John."

"We'll work on that later," the colonel said, taking him by the arm. "Tonight you need to forget your troubles, and I have just the lady to help. Come with me."

Edward allowed his host to lead him across the ballroom, concealing his reluctance and bracing himself to do the pretty with whatever insipid young lady to whom he was introduced. The colonel escorted him to a group of chairs by the wall where a young dark-haired woman in yellow sat with an older woman in purple silk.

"Lady Juliette Blackwood, I should like to present Captain Edward Tremaine, an old acquaintance of mine, as a suitable partner for the next dance," Colonel Wentworth said with the air of one bestowing a great favour.

Edward's reluctance to dance vanished as Lady Juliette Blackwood smiled up at him. She was breathtakingly beautiful—gleaming black hair hung in curls about a delicate oval face, and her pale yellow muslin dress clung to her limbs and outlined a slender figure that was perfection. Long black eyelashes fluttered briefly over deep blue eyes, and her red lips continued to smile as she acknowledged the introduction.

"Captain Tremaine," she said, "I am pleased to make your acquaintance. May I present you to my brother, Viscount Blackwood, and my aunt, Lady Martin."

Edward bowed to Lord Blackwood, a male version of Lady Juliette standing behind her chair, and kissed the hand of the stern-looking older woman sitting next to Lady Juliette, but he barely saw them and did not register their replies. In a daze he led Lady Juliette out onto the floor. As they lined up for the country dance, he was suddenly glad he had ordered new coats from Weston upon arriving in Town, and was looking at least passable in silk knee breeches and a well-fitted coat of claret kerseymere.

The figures of the dance allowed them little time to converse, and after the dance he was reluctant to leave Lady Juliette's presence without learning more about her. He asked if he could procure some lemonade for the two women, planning to stay and talk as they drank it.

Lady Juliette was quite willing to converse, and as she sipped her lemonade she asked Edward many questions about his family and their estate in Sussex. He answered her questions gladly, staying with Lady Juliette and her aunt until another partner claimed her. Then, reluctantly recognising that he had been monopolising Lady Juliette, he took his leave, but not before obtaining a promise from her to go for a walk in the Park the next morning.

The anticipation of seeing Lady Juliette again the next day acted as a tonic on Edward, and he spent the rest of the evening dancing every dance, impervious to fatigue. Mrs. Wentworth decided her husband's friend was the perfect guest, for he willingly led out even the most unattractive of the young women, and no one languished by the wall.

In the early hours of the morning he returned happily to Stephen's Hotel in Bond Street, thinking of Lady Juliette. She was the kind of woman a man dreamed of but never really thought to meet. She was beautiful, charming, witty and, he felt sure, talented in many ways. Now he was sorry he had planned to return to the country next week. Perhaps he could delay his departure.

THE NEXT MORNING, at their marginally fashionable address in Marylebone, Lord Adrian Blackwood talked with his sister as she waited for Captain Tremaine to collect her for their walk in the Park.

"Why are you wasting time on a mere Captain Tremaine, my dear?" drawled Adrian, leaning negligently against the fireplace and tapping his gleaming Hessians with his whip. "He is not even well favoured."

Lady Blackwood frowned at her brother with irritation.

"He's heir to a viscountcy, and I haven't seen anything better," she replied, a calculating expression on her face that looked oddly incongruous with the fresh picture she presented in her white muslin. "His appearance is regrettable, but beggars can't be choosers." She looked at the frayed and worn upholstery of the furniture in their rented town house with distaste.

"You were supposed to find someone suitable for me and haven't," she accused, an aggrieved edge to her voice.

"That, dear sister, is your doing," Lord Blackwood replied, yawning lazily. "If you hadn't spent a night on the road in the company of Lord Crawford last Season you would not have cast doubt upon your reputation. Now men are willing to dance attendance upon your beauty, but won't come up to scratch."

"I told you nothing happened," Lady Juliette said, scowling at her brother. "If Lady Parkenham hadn't chanced to be at the same inn and seen us having supper together in the private parlour, no one would have been the wiser. Spiteful old cat. She always hated me because I outshone her fubsy-faced daughter the year of our come-outs."

Lady Juliette frowned more deeply at the memories, lines marring the satin smoothness of her forehead, and then changed from defense to attack.

"If you hadn't gambled away what little we had, it wouldn't be necessary for me to marry for money. Speaking of marrying for money, why don't you do so yourself?" she demanded with asperity. "Your reputation is even worse, that's why."

Lady Juliette paused a moment to glare angrily at her brother, but Lord Blackwood, used to his sister's temper, merely smiled aggravatingly. She looked away, picking up a Worcester figurine of a lady in blue from the table next to her, turning it around in her slender hands.

"Captain Tremaine will have to do. He is well-to-pass if not wealthy. I intend to wrangle an invitation to his family's estate in Sussex when he returns there. London is thin of company in the summer, and I'm not likely to find anyone better at this date. If you don't wish to accompany me, you may join our esteemed father on the Continent. I can't afford to rent these lodgings for your convenience."

Lord Blackwood made no immediate comment. He straightened and walked to the window, pushing aside the grimy draperies with his whip in order to have a better view of the street.

"I might as well accompany you to Sussex. Perhaps there will be a country heiress who has not heard of my reputation, and you will not have to sacrifice yourself on a mere Captain Tremaine, after all. Here comes your victim now," he added letting the draperies fall back. "I shall have Aunt join you. You had best work fast while he is infatuated and get him safely back to Sussex before someone enlightens him as to your slightly tarnished reputation."

He exited with a smile at his glaring sister, who clutched the figurine tightly. Only the fact that there was not enough time to clean up the mess before Captain Tremaine was shown into the drawing room kept her from flinging it at her brother's departing back.

JANE SIGHED as she sorted through her father's voluminous correspondence. Nothing for her amongst it. He had not said he would, but Jane had harboured hopes that Edward would send her a letter from London while he was there. Surely that would not have been improper, given the friendship between the families. It had been fully two weeks since he had left, and there had been no word. Not even Lady Tremaine had heard from him. Jane took the offending letters in to her father, who was so absorbed in his work that he barely noted her presence until she started to leave.

"Jane, would you help me with my latest chapter this morning? I need your fair hand for the final copy," he said flatteringly.

"I cannot help you this morning. I promised to go riding with Fanny and Lord Grandville, but I shall have time to make a copy this afternoon," Jane promised.

Mr. Hampton looked up from his desk. "Lord Grandville has become a frequent caller, has he not?"

"Yes, he has shown a definite interest in Fanny's company."

"Perhaps it is time Fanny officially ended her betrothal to James Tremaine. Although he has been a frequent caller also, hasn't he?" Mr. Hampton sighed at the thought of having to disrupt his studies to deal with a family problem. He much preferred his world of books. So much more orderly.

"Don't worry about Fanny, Papa," Jane said to allay her father's worry. "I believe Fanny is quite capable of dealing with both Jamie and Lord Grandville properly."

Pleased to be relieved of his responsibilities so easily, Mr. Hampton picked up his pen and returned to his work.

"Mind you leave the afternoon free," he admonished as she left the room.

"Yes, Papa," she promised. Helping her father with his work more frequently had helped her not to miss Captain Tremaine so much, but it had its disadvantages. The more she assisted him, the more he required her presence.

She was on her way upstairs when she heard Fanny's voice calling after her.

"Jane, hurry and get dressed or you will not be ready when Lord Grandville arrives."

"I'm on my way now. Don't fret," Jane said, turning to her sister, who stood at the bottom of the stairs looking at her anxiously. She was fetching, clad in a carriage dress of apricot muslin and a cottage bonnet trimmed with blond lace. Jane smiled at her reassuringly and hurried on upstairs to her bedchamber.

Jane reflected that one thing she had to be grateful for lately was Fanny's rapid return to health. She seemed to have accepted her changed appearance and decided to make the best of it. No doubt the attention she was receiving from several men had something to do with it. Jamie and Chris came often, and Jane was amused by Jamie's sudden willingness to keep up the pretense of the betrothal. He acted quite possessively, glaring at Chris when he was there and sulking when Lord Grandville appeared. Fanny seemed to accept Jamie's presence with equanimity, however. Jane wondered what she was planning to do about the betrothal. She seemed to have no interest in continuing it, and might wish to be free to receive attentions from Chris or Lord Grandville.

She went to her wardrobe and plucked out a dress at random. She had become accustomed to the daily visits from Edward, and found life sadly flat with him gone. Playing chaperone to her sister was not the same as having her company sought for itself.

"Jane, Lord Grandville is here. Hurry," Fanny's voice called. Jane took a bonnet from the shelf of her wardrobe and hastened down the stairs. She tried to throw off her melancholy lest she be a poor companion for the other two, and smiled charmingly at Lord

Grandville as he stood beside his carriage to hand them up.

He was assisting Jane into the carriage while his groom held the horses when a second equipage drove up. It was a fashionable perch phaeton in a glossy orange lacquer drawn by matched chestnuts caparisoned in rosettes and ribands. Jamie himself was dressed to the nines in a canary coat, pea-green pantaloons, purple waistcoat and a white neckcloth.

"I say, Fanny," he called, looking at Lord Grandville's old-fashioned carriage in disparagement, "*I* was going to take you for a drive this morning."

"I'm sorry, Jamie, I don't recall your asking me," Fanny replied, as Jane settled herself on the seat of Lord Grandville's carriage.

"Jane can go with Lord Grandville and you can come with me," Jamie insisted as the earl held his hand out for Fanny.

Jane saw Fanny hesitate, unsure what to do. If she refused, it would look odd to those watching from behind the curtains of the village cottages, since Jamie was supposedly still her betrothed. But Jane knew Fanny would much prefer to go with Lord Grandville.

Lord Grandville sensed her dilemma, and said in a low voice, "It's all right, Miss Fanny. Go with him this morning and I will take you tomorrow."

"You are the winner this morning, Tremaine," he said pleasantly as he helped Fanny into the phaeton, but Jamie rudely turned his head away and made no answer.

Fanny watched in envy as the earl drove off with Jane. "Really, Jamie, that was beyond anything. I had a commitment to the earl," she said with irritation.

"It's not the thing for you to be driving out with other men when you are betrothed to me," Jamie responded truculently as the phaeton began to move.

Fanny looked at him measuringly. "I am *not* betrothed to you, as you well know."

"Well, others don't know, and it looks deuced shabby for you to be receiving so much attention from other men," he said as his chestnuts began to pick up speed.

Fanny's temper began to rise at this dressing down. "I think it is time we officially ended our betrothal. Then you can have no objections to my behaviour."

"Don't fly up into the boughs so." Jamie turned to look at Fanny and said almost hesitantly, "I've been meaning to say, Fan, we needn't end the betrothal at all. We could go on as before."

Fanny was angry at his assumption that she would care to continue her betrothal to him after his treatment of her. She opened her mouth to tell him what she thought when she caught a fleeting glimpse of the old Jamie in the boyish face. Her anger died, and she answered mildly.

"No, Jamie, we can't go on as before. It is not possible after what happened."

"Are you going to hold that against a fellow forever?" Jamie pleaded. "I had had a shock."

Fanny didn't try to explain that her appearance when she was ill should not have revolted him if he had loved her. Shocked him perhaps, but not revolted him.

"I think it best we end it, Jamie," she repeated.

"I know what it is," he said sullenly, flicking the horses lightly with his whip to increase their speed. "You're hoping to snabble the earl. That's much better than the younger son of a viscount. Why else would you see so much of that . . . that macaroni."

Fanny knew it was Jamie's wounded vanity speaking, but the benevolent feeling toward him she had just experienced vanished completely.

"Don't you dare speak to me that way," she said as the phaeton careened on at a faster and faster pace. "Not after your Turkish treatment of me when I was ill. I want the betrothal ended."

"I refuse!" he shouted to her, whipping up the horses until the phaeton swayed dangerously going around a curve, bringing him back to his senses. He slowed the horses and Fanny demanded to be taken home. Sullenly he obliged, and they returned without speaking. Fanny was ready to jump off the phaeton immediately it stopped by the gate, but caught herself as she saw how far above the ground she was. Fortunately, Ned Reid was watching for her return and ran to help her down, allowing her to walk off with dignity.

Jane fared better on her drive with the earl, although she knew it was her sister's company that he had desired. He was an amusing companion and his sharp observations on human nature and his comments on the country society he had recently become a part of kept her diverted until they returned.

However, the drive had failed to raise her spirits entirely, and it was with a long face that she joined her sister in the garden where she was sipping a glass of lemonade.

Fanny was still seething from Jamie's behaviour during the drive.

"Would you believe Jamie asked me to let our betrothal stand?" she demanded of Jane, her eyes flashing.

"No! How could he?" Jane said indignantly, her own troubles forgotten. "You refused, of course."

"Yes, but he refused to end it officially. I shall have to speak to Lady Tremaine about it, and I had not wished to distress her."

Once she had given vent to her indignation, her anger cooled slightly.

"Actually, I felt sorry for him for a moment," she confessed. "I suppose to a Pink of the Ton like Jamie, my appearance that day *was* quite shocking. But if that was his reaction to my losing my looks now, when it was only temporary, what would he do when they change as I get older? Keep mistresses? I know that is the custom with men of his class, but I shouldn't like it."

Jane was rather shocked at Fanny's plain speaking, but she had to acknowledge she made a legitimate point.

"It's odd how different Edward is from his brother," Jane said musingly.

Fanny's attention was caught by the words and the tone of Jane's voice. She looked at her with concern.

"Jane," said Fanny hesitantly, "what are your feelings for Captain Tremaine? You have developed a *tendre* for him, haven't you?"

Jane blushed and took another sip of lemonade, hoping her feelings were not as visible to others as they evidently were to her sister.

"Yes, I suppose I have," she admitted rather reluctantly. Admitting it to someone made it seem somehow tenuous and fragile.

Fanny was silent a moment, and then said cautiously, "I don't know how to say this, but are you sure Captain Tremaine returns your affections?"

Jane took umbrage at Fanny's question. She might not wish others to discover what her feelings were until Edward spoke, but she knew he *would* speak. It was just a matter of time. Surely he would speak by the end of the summer.

"He has not spoken yet, if that is what you want to know, but yes, he has given me reason to think that he holds me in affection."

Fanny put a hand on Jane's arm. "Don't be angry," Fanny pleaded. "I am just trying to spare you the pain I suffered. I have observed you and Captain Tremaine together. He does appear to hold you in affection, but it seemed to me to be a sisterly affection, not anything more."

Jane was contrite. "I am sorry, Fanny. But I think you are worried about me needlessly. Edward *has* given me reason to think my affections are returned, I assure you."

Fanny said no more, and they sat together quietly until they finished their lemonade.

Jane tried to dismiss the doubt Fanny's words had caused, but as she copied the chapters for her father that afternoon, she found her mind wandering from its task, and she had to copy several sheets over. Edward *did* care for her. He must! Why else would he kiss her and ask her to call him by his given name? He was not like Jamie, to blow hot and cold and trifle with one's affections.

ST. JAMES PARK was refreshingly cool after the crowded boxes of the Little Theatre at Haymarket. Both Drury Lane and Covent Garden Theatre were closed after being burned down, and the Little Theatre had had a great crush of people attending.

Edward bent his head to look at Lady Juliette, and his heart contracted as she bestowed one of her brilliant smiles upon him. She looked enchanting—beautifully innocent in white muslin, a simple necklace of sapphires and a plain white bandeau in her hair. She was not as elaborately dressed as many of the women at the theatre had been, but Edward felt the simplicity of her toilette made the others look overdone. He had no way of knowing that the only reason Lady Juliette dressed simply in sapphires was because she had been forced to sell her more expensive pearls and diamonds last Season. Her aunt, Lady Martin, walked silently beside them.

"May we rest a moment before we return to the carriage?" Lady Juliette asked as they came to some benches located by beds of colourful flowers.

"Of course. How thoughtless of me," Edward said, leading Lady Juliette and her aunt to a bench under the shade of a tree.

"London is excessively hot in the summer, is it not?" Lady Juliette asked, opening her fan and waving it gently before her face, smiling up at him beguilingly.

"Yes, it is much more comfortable in the country," Edward replied, and wondered if he dared put the plan he had come up with to the test.

"Of course, you normally spend summers at your estate. I hope I am not keeping you from your family, Captain Tremaine?"

"No, but it *is* time I returned to Haverton Park." He took a deep breath and plunged in. "Might I hope you would accompany me back to Haverton Park, Lady Juliette? And you also, Lady Martin," he added, inclining his head to that lady. "And your brother, of course."

Lady Juliette turned away as though in confusion, and Edward missed the brief gleam of triumph in her eyes and the satisfied smile that touched her lips.

"Thank you, Captain Tremaine. We should be pleased to accompany you to Sussex," she replied. "Shouldn't we, Aunt?"

"Yes, it is kind of you to extend the invitation," Lady Martin answered with a barely visible smile.

Edward felt a joy he could barely contain at the idea of spending a summer in the company of someone as beautiful and charming as Lady Juliette. He could hardly wait for his family to meet her, and Jane, of course. He envisioned Jane and Lady Juliette's becoming the best of friends.

CHAPTER SIX

JANE KNELT IN HER GARDEN, wearing an old cotton print dress and deep-brimmed cottage bonnet, pulling weeds and picking off dead flower heads. Most of the roses were gone, but the midsummer blooms were starting. The lupine, lamb's ears and a few late peonies made a pretty show of colour, and the alyssum and mignonette released a sun-sweet scent.

"I knew I would find you here in your garden," a voice called from the gate.

"Edward," Jane cried, jumping up and going eagerly toward him, a feeling of joy coursing through her.

Edward entered the gate and clasped both Jane's hands in his own. Jane noticed immediately how much better he looked. Although he was still slim, his frame had filled out and his blond hair shone healthily in the sunlight. He was wearing new clothes, evidently cut by a city tailor. The blue coat hugged his shoulders closely, and the fawn-coloured pantaloons fit as tightly as any of Jamie's. The trip to London seemed to have done him a world of good.

"How did things go?" she asked, hoping his cheerful visage presaged success. "Did you succeed in getting someone to listen to you about Sir John Moore?"

Edward's cheerful expression dimmed and was replaced by a sombre look. He released her hands and ran his fingers through his hair in the gesture Jane had come to associate with frustration.

"I am afraid that part of my trip did not go well. A friend of mine, Colonel Wentworth, obtained audiences for me with both Castlereagh and Canning, but neither would listen. I fear Lord Grandville was correct that they had made a scapegoat of Sir John. I don't know what I can do now," he finished, "although Colonel Wentworth has promised to write if he can find out anything for me. I can only wait.

"But," he resumed, his face lightening, "I have some good news I have been anxious to tell you."

"What's that?" Jane asked, smiling at the boyishly eager expression on his face.

"I've brought guests back to Haverton Park. Oh, Jane," he said, "I have met the most beautiful woman—Lady Juliette Blackwood. And I owe it all to you for sending me to London."

Jane felt the smile freeze on her face as she struggled not to let the shock she felt show. She evidently succeeded, for Edward continued his panegyric on the charms of Lady Juliette without a pause, although his exact words of praise did not register on Jane's numbed brain. Finally a sentence penetrated her consciousness.

"Mother is planning a ball in four days to introduce Lady Juliette and her brother to the neighbourhood.

You must come. I am most anxious for you to meet Lady Juliette. I know you will like her."

"We shall be pleased to come," Jane answered automatically, thinking desperately how she could avoid it. "Now come inside and tell Fanny your news," she added, leading the way into the cottage, glad for an excuse to turn her face away.

Fanny was working on some embroidery in the drawing room and laid it aside as Edward repeated his news for her ears. Fanny asked several questions, covering Jane's silence. Indeed, Jane felt Fanny was purposely distracting his attention from her and was grateful. She could not have spoken naturally if her life depended upon it. Fortunately Edward did not stay long, being anxious to return to Haverton Park and his guests.

When he had gone, Jane was unable to control her emotions any longer. She clenched her jaws together to keep the sobs back, but the tears began to roll down her cheeks despite all her efforts. Fanny put her arms about Jane and led her to the settee, drawing her down and holding her close as Jane's shoulders shook with sobs.

"Fanny, what can I do? I can't go to the ball and face Edward's intended," Jane cried.

"You must," Fanny replied firmly but compassionately. "What did you tell me about facing Jamie? It will not be as difficult as you fear. Oh, Jane," she said in distress, "I did try to spare you this."

Jane did not answer. She knew now Fanny had been right, but she had felt so sure that Edward's warmth towards her before he left for London had indicated the development of strong feelings. How could she have been so mistaken? Had it all been wishful thinking on her part? As her misery deepened, the tears ceased to fall, but her throat felt constricted, and her whole chest ached.

Fanny, worried, went to get some tea, leaving Jane staring blindly at the floor.

She felt betrayed by Edward, even though she had to recognise now that the warmth he had demonstrated towards her, even the light kisses on her forehead, had been no more than what a brother might demonstrate towards a sister he held in affection. It was not his fault she had misinterpreted his actions.

Fanny returned with the tea, pressing a cup into Jane's hands and talking soothingly. When she had drunk it, Fanny led Jane upstairs to her bedchamber and persuaded her to lie down. Jane gave in, preferring to be left alone with her dark thoughts. Perhaps if she gave in to them fully they would soon leave.

Several hours later, Jane washed her face and went back downstairs, determined to show at least equal courage to that which Fanny had shown when she faced Jamie for the first time since her illness. She would attend the ball and meet Edward's guests proudly.

She asked Fanny's help in selecting a dress for the ball. At least she could do as Fanny had and gain some measure of confidence by looking well. The ball was four days off, and there was no time to make a new dress, but she could refurbish an old one. She knew that only the confidence that came from knowing she looked her best would give her the strength to get through the ball.

She and Fanny walked to the village shops to get new ribands and embroidery silks, and Jane turned them over to the capable hands of Mrs. Reid. Fortunately, Edward's guests kept him at Haverton Park. Jane had never thought to be relieved the morning talks with Edward were not resumed, but she was.

THE NIGHT OF THE BALL, Jane assessed her appearance with satisfaction. The V-neck frock of white sarcenet with its short puffed sleeves flattered her, and the fringed stole embroidered in shades of green and coral draped gracefully across her shoulders provided just the right touch. She wore matching coral silk gloves and slippers and carried a pale green silk fan with ivory guards. A simple coral necklace adorned her throat, and she fastened a coral-coloured rose in her hair with a white riband. She knew she was looking her best, and turned to thank Mrs. Reid and Fanny with relief and gratitude.

Fanny was also in excellent looks. She had chosen a trained white muslin dress with a rounded bodice *à l'enfant*, and wore an India shawl of pastels. A simple cabochon pendant rested above her breasts, and a matching carnelian brooch fastened her riband belt. Fanny still missed her silver-blond tresses, but the soft curls *à la Titus* set off with an ostrich feather looked very fetching.

Lord Grandville had offered to collect the Hamptons in his large carriage, and it bolstered Jane's confidence to arrive in company with the earl. Even so, as they entered the hall of Haverton Park, her heart began to beat quickly with nervousness.

Edward stood with his guests at the door of the ballroom. The Archers had arrived just before the Hamptons, and as they waited their turn to be presented, Jane had the opportunity to look at Lady Juliette Blackwood unobserved. Her heart sank, and she was no longer as satisfied with her own appearance as she realised that Edward had not exaggerated Lady Juliette's beauty. Her shining black hair was dressed *à la Sappho*, its glossiness emphasised by the white silk ribands threaded through the long curls. She was clad in a white silk gown edged in trim of a Greek motif, and a necklace of garnets shone darkly at her throat. Embroidered satin slippers peeped from beneath her hem, and she held a fan of garnet-coloured silk.

Owing to her close scrutiny of Lady Juliette, Jane could detect a brief flash of astonishment on Lady Juliette's face as her attention was caught by Lord Grandville's appearance. He was clad tonight in a formal suit of figured lilac silk with an ornately embroidered yellow waistcoat, a powdered curled periwig and high-heeled buckled shoes. A jewel-hilted dress sword dangled at his side, and a large emerald ring adorned his hand.

Although the look on Lady Juliette's face had passed in a moment, the earl had noticed it, too. Turning towards Jane and Fanny, he gave them a barely perceptible wink. As Lady Juliette was presented to Lord Grandville, he bowed over her hand in what was almost a parody of the old style.

"Zounds," he drawled, looking Lady Juliette up and down, "sink me if it ain't Artemis come to life. Fair vision! To torment us mortals," he said, sweeping another elaborate bow.

Jane heard a choking sound from Fanny and knew she was trying hard not to laugh. Jane had not missed the speculative gleam in Lady Juliette's eyes as she discovered the quiz in the outmoded clothes was an earl, and she rather thought the earl had not missed it, either.

The earl's teasing of Lady Juliette gave Jane the courage to meet her calmly. As she was presented, she noted that Lady Blackwood was even more beautiful close up. Long dark eyelashes swept over clear blue eyes, and her red lips and cheeks owed nothing to artifice.

Lady Juliette greeted Jane politely but dismissively, and passed her to her brother, Lord Blackwood. In her preoccupation with the sister, Jane had not noticed Lord Blackwood before, but now she saw he was as handsome as Lady Juliette was beautiful. He was clad in tight cassimere breeches, a fine lace-trimmed shirt, buff waistcoat and a form-fitting coat of blue superfine. He had the same black hair and blue eyes as his sister, but where her expression was demure, his was almost devilish. The deep blue eyes swept over her boldly and appreciatively.

"Captain Tremaine did not tell me what beauty was to be found in the country, or I would have persuaded him to return to Sussex much sooner," Lord Blackwood said, bowing over Jane's hand. "Promise me you will save the first dance for me, Miss Hampton."

Jane, pleased to be so noticed, agreed, happy that the informality of a country ball did not force those of high rank to dance first with others of equal rank. At least she would be seen to dance the first dance with the most handsome man present tonight. Excepting Edward, she added to herself, glancing back wistfully at his fair countenance.

Jane and Fanny went into the ballroom and looked for Lady Archer. Mr. Hampton had an unhappy propensity for disappearing into his host's library, and either Lady Archer or Lady Tremaine functioned as Jane and Fanny's chaperone at neighbourhood entertainments. They spied Lady Archer and Marianne sitting on gilt chairs next to the south wall and went to join them.

Lord Blackwood claimed Jane's hand promptly for the first dance. He was an excellent dancer, and Jane thoroughly enjoyed standing up with him, though her enjoyment was moderated when she saw Lady Juliette and Edward dancing together not far away. They looked striking together, she had to admit, the one so fair and the other so dark. She looked back to Lord Blackwood and thought she saw a flash of compassion in his eyes, but he only complimented her on her grace in dancing and praised the Tremaines' hospitality.

When Lord Blackwood returned her to Lady Archer's side, he requested her promise to save him another dance, and she willingly agreed. Jane's second dance was claimed by Christopher, and her third, the one she dreaded, by Edward. She had no wish to hear more encomiums on Lady Juliette.

"Tell me, Jane," he demanded as soon as the figures of the dance allowed them to speak, "what do you think of Lady Juliette? Isn't she all I told you she was?"

Jane, Juliette. Jane could hear the difference in his voice as he spoke the names, and it tore at her heart.

"Yes," she answered honestly, "she is most beautiful and charming."

"I knew you would agree," Edward said happily. "Your approval means a great deal to me. I am counting on you and Fanny to help me entertain Lady Juliette and her brother during their stay," he added. "I thought we would plan some excursions and ride together mornings."

Jane demurred. It was one thing to be polite occasionally to the woman Edward had chosen instead of herself, it was another to be forced to be intimate with her and watch Edward courting her.

"Perhaps we shall be able to join you sometimes," she said cautiously, "but my father is nearing the completion of his book and requires my assistance rather more frequently than before. Besides, I am not at all a good horsewoman."

"I am sure your father will excuse you sometimes," Edward said. "As for your riding, I still am not strong enough to handle my father's spirited mounts and plan to ride Ariel. You would surely be able to keep up with him."

Jane smiled in response to his teasing, but remained noncommittal. After the dance he restored her to Lady Archer and left to find his next partner. Jamie had just escorted Fanny to Lady Archer's side and was looking disgruntled. He spied Jane and claimed her next dance. Jane wished she might refuse, as she sensed he wished to speak to her about Fanny, but good manners would not allow her to do so.

Jamie was dressed more conservatively than usual tonight, in black silk breeches, white dimity waistcoat, a wine-coloured coat and a simple white stock with a black riband tied around it. If it had not been for the profusion of fobs that dangled over the top of his breeches, he would have looked quite elegant, Jane thought in surprise.

As she expected, he spoke to her of Fanny as soon as they walked onto the floor.

"Miss Hampton, couldn't you speak to your sister? I wish to set a date for our wedding, but Fanny persists in wanting to cry off."

"The decision is Fanny's. I would not think of trying to influence her," she said rather mendaciously, thinking that if Fanny had shown any interest in continuing the betrothal she would have done her best to persuade her otherwise.

"Perhaps the thing would be to allow it to be broken off, and then try to win her back," she suggested.

"Wouldn't do at all," Jamie said glumly. "The minute she's free of me she'll go to the earl," he said, looking to where Fanny and Lord Grandville were dancing together for the second time.

"Then perhaps you should call it off. Surely you don't want Fanny if she prefers another man," Jane ventured, keeping her voice very low so they would not be overheard.

Jamie looked at her disgustedly and dropped the subject. She hoped he would not plague Fanny excessively about the betrothal. It would be distressful for her if she had to speak to Lady Tremaine about his conduct.

Jane enjoyed the evening more than she had hoped, because of the attention of Lord Blackwood, but was relieved when she saw Squire Shirley and his wife take their leave, and knew she and Fanny could also. She signalled to Fanny and they went to search for their father. As they expected, they found him ensconced in a comfortable chair in Lord Tremaine's well-stocked library.

"Is it that late already?" he asked in surprise, his eyes going to the long case clock in the corner of the room. "I suppose it is," he said with a sigh, regretfully putting down his book and reluctantly accompanying his daughters home.

THE AFTERNOON FOLLOWING the ball, Jane and Fanny received a note from Haverton Park requesting they meet Edward and his guests there the next morning to go riding. Jane did not want to go, but realised she had no valid excuse to stay away. She was not being modest when she said she was no horsewoman, and she felt sure somehow that Lady Juliette would be. Fanny's skill was little better than Jane's, but she was game to go. They searched out their little-used riding habits and gave them to Mrs. Reid to press.

Early the next morning they walked to the stables at Haverton Park where they found the others already gathered. Jane and Fanny requested gentle mounts, and Edward had two small mares brought out for them. Lord Blackwood helped Jane to mount as Edward assisted Lady Juliette onto a spirited gelding.

Lady Juliette was wearing a beautiful habit of yellow velvet trimmed in black military braid, and she had a dashing hat set on her dusky curls. Jane felt outlandishly dowdy in her brown cloth habit, and resigned herself to what she felt sure would be a miserable ride. They set out in twos, Edward with Lady Juliette, Fanny with Jamie, and Jane and Lord Blackwood bringing up the rear.

They had not gone far when they encountered Lord Grandville on a large grey. He was clad in old-style riding clothes, consisting of leather breeches, a scarlet waistcoat, laced hat and jackboots. He was invited to join their group, and the addition of his spirited horse made the others resent the slow pace, moving the earl to suggest a short gallop to the Blackwoods. Lord Blackwood declined, but Lady Juliette accepted eagerly. The two gave their mounts their heads, and soon vanished from sight.

When the rest of the party caught up with them, Lady Juliette was laughing up at the earl as their horses walked along slowly, their energy spent. A momentary frown crossed Edward's face, but it disappeared when Lady Juliette became aware of their presence and rode up to him.

"We had the most glorious gallop, Edward. You needn't refuse yourself the pleasure of one to stay with Miss Hampton and Miss Fanny. I am sure my brother is willing to bear them company."

Jane kept her expression neutral, but she was appalled by Lady Juliette's insensitivity. Couldn't the lady see that Edward stayed with them, not only out of good manners, but also because he was not up to a gallop yet? Jane could not believe a woman could be so unaware of his feelings. He could not like having it pointed out to the others that he was still so weak.

But Edward did not seem to take offense. "I am afraid I am not yet up to the rigours of a gallop, Lady Juliette. I must forgo the pleasure until I have regained more of my strength. Until then I am glad the presence of Lord Grandville keeps you from being denied your exercise."

"Odds boots and spurs," Lord Grandville replied, sweeping off his gold-laced hat gallantly. "I am pleased to be of service to such a Vision of Beauty."

Jane wondered at Lord Grandville's continuing to speak to Lady Juliette in the overdone fashion of the 1770s. She saw Edward give the earl a sharp look, as though he wondered at it, too, but he made no comment.

Lord Grandville and Lady Juliette rode off ahead, and Jane completed the ride in Edward's company, but she got little pleasure from it. He spent most of his time gazing after Lady Juliette. Like a mooncalf, Jane thought uncharitably, and was relieved when the ride was over. Edward pressed Jane and Fanny to stay at Haverton Park and visit with his guests, but Jane refused, protesting they could not remain in their riding clothes. Edward accepted this excuse, but insisted that they return that afternoon, a request seconded by Jamie and Lord Blackwood. Realising she could not refuse without appearing uncivil, Jane had to agree.

WHEN JANE AND FANNY returned to Haverton Park that afternoon, they found Lord Grandville, the Blackwoods and Lady Tremaine assembled in the Green Drawing Room. Lady Juliette had changed into a cambric round gown of a blue that matched her eyes. She was arguing with Lady Tremaine in an animated fashion. As Jane and Fanny were announced by Dawkins, she turned to them with a smile.

"Here, Miss Hampton, you must resolve our argument. I say that *Marmion* is the better of Mr. Scott's works, but Lady Tremaine claims it cannot match *The Lay of the Last Minstrel.*"

"You must ask my sister, Fanny," Jane replied, smiling, sitting on a green brocade upholstered chair near the window. "I must confess I have read neither."

Lady Juliette's eyebrows rose fractionally. "You speak seriously, Miss Hampton? You have not read Mr. Scott's works?"

"How very peculiar," Lady Martin sniffed, her high-bridged nose lifting higher.

"My sister has no time for light works," defended Fanny. "She assists our father with his studies. He is a scholar."

"Oh, a bluestocking," Lady Juliette replied, her tone saying that explained everything. Jane flushed, wishing she had stayed away whether it would have been rude or not. Lady Juliette had the knack of making her feel like a backward provincial.

"Faith, can't say I've read them m'self," Lord Grandville interposed. "Odds meters and rhymes, I say there's no equal to Cunninghame.

'I'll wear thy colours in my cap,
  Thy picture at my heart,
And he that bends not to thine eye
  Shall rue it to his smart!'"

Having thus quoted from the eighteenth-century poet, he looked at Lady Juliette meaningfully.

Lady Juliette's attention was successfully diverted from Jane's shortcomings, and a discussion of favourite poets ensued.

"Tell me, Miss Hampton," a voice spoke softly in her ear, "does our Sir Lucius O'Trigger always speak so, or is it for my sister's benefit?"

Jane turned smilingly to Lord Blackwood, who had come to stand behind her chair. She was glad she did not have to confess ignorance of Lord Blackwood's allusion. Fortunately she had seen *The Rivals* performed in Bath. Lord Grandville *did* sound rather like O'Trigger, she thought, diverted.

"You needn't answer," he said, watching the thoughts play across her face, "we shall soon see."

Lord Blackwood expertly coaxed Jane out of her megrims, and she soon forgot Lady Juliette's scorn and enjoyed the rest of the afternoon. The group arranged to meet to ride together every morning, and Lord Grandville suggested a picnic on the grounds of his estate, Bramleigh. The suggestion was received with enthusiasm by everyone, and it was set for three days hence.

As Jane and Fanny walked back to Staplefield, Fanny teased Jane about Lord Blackwood's attentions.

"I suppose you are going to tell me they are just brotherly," Jane said rather sarcastically, beginning to walk faster.

"No," Fanny said, "the looks he gives you are far from brotherly."

Jane felt herself blush. "I wonder why Lord Grandville persists in speaking in that ridiculous fashion to Lady Juliette," she said to change the subject. "Even Lord Blackwood noticed it."

"Wasn't it delicious," Fanny gurgled.

"But perhaps a little unkind," Jane said. "Everyone knows he is making a Maygame of her."

"Fustian. She brings his teasing upon herself," Fanny said. "To think of what she said to you. That was unkind."

Jane made no reply, for although it was not becoming in a former vicar's daughter, she *had* been glad for Lord Grandville's teasing of Lady Juliette.

They walked along in silence for a while, Fanny with a thoughtful expression on her face.

"I don't think Juliette would be the right wife for Captain Tremaine," Fanny said as they neared their cottage. "I cannot like her."

"She is beautiful and charming, and of high rank," Jane stated calmly.

"Perhaps. I shall concede that. But I wager she only likes Captain Tremaine because he is heir to a viscountcy. Lord Grandville tells me there is some question about her reputation, and that of her brother, also."

"You shouldn't be discussing such things with the earl. It's not proper," Jane said automatically.

Fanny ignored her. "You would be a better wife for Captain Tremaine, if he could see beyond his nose. If he saw the true colours of Lady Juliette he would not think they were pretty."

"It is none of our affair what Captain Tremaine does," Jane said sternly. "You were correct when you told me Captain Tremaine only regarded me as a sister. I must accept that. You are not to interfere."

Fanny only smiled enigmatically, and Jane felt uneasy. She had longed for Fanny's mischievousness to return, but in the past that expression had always presaged trouble.

CHAPTER SEVEN

THE NEXT MORNING, Jane began her usual chore of sorting through her father's correspondence and putting it in piles according to the subjects addressed. As she performed her routine task, her attention was caught by the name Sir John Moore mentioned in a letter from the Bishop of Salisbury.

"Would the brother of the Bishop of Salisbury have connections, Papa?" she asked as she scanned the letter.

"What, my dear?" her father asked, taking off his spectacles and looking up reluctantly from his papers.

"The Bishop of Salisbury mentions his brother, Colonel Fisher, in reference to Sir John Moore." She went on to explain Edward's futile attempts to restore the name of his commander. "Perhaps the brother of the bishop would have connections Edward does not."

"Why don't you give Captain Tremaine his direction, then?"

Jane was thoughtful. "Perhaps it would be better if you would write first, Papa. I should hate to get Captain Tremaine's hopes up if nothing should come of it. He was quite cast down when his efforts in London came to nothing."

Her father agreed. "Give me the letter, dear, while I remember. If you wish it, I shall write directly. If the bishop should not be able to help we shall not tell Captain Tremaine of our attempt."

Jane thanked her father and kissed him affectionately before going back to her task.

THAT SAME MORNING, Edward found he had a moment for himself while Lady Juliette changed from her riding clothes and Lord Blackwood rode to Staplefield with Jamie. The one thing he was finding disagreeable about his guests was that they required his full attention. He could not leave them to their own devices often, for Lady Juliette and her aunt were not generally disposed towards quiet pastimes.

He sighed. It was more than a week since he had returned from London, and he had not yet had a chance to discuss his trip with his father. He wanted to tell him that his attempts to interest someone in London on behalf of Sir John had been futile and apply to him for his advice. Perhaps he could find him now, he thought, looking at the clock. At this time of the morning he might be able to find his father in his study.

Viscount Tremaine was indeed in his study. He sat behind his satinwood desk frowning in concentration at his account books.

"May I disturb you a moment?" Edward asked, coming into the room and going to stand before his father's desk. "I wished to ask your advice on what I can do about clearing Sir John's name."

Viscount Tremaine set his accounts aside and looked thoughtfully at his son, motioning him to be seated.

"I take it, then, that that part of your journey was not successful?"

"No," Edward replied, relaxing thankfully into a comfortable chair. "I don't know what to do. Castlereagh and Canning were the highest-ranking politicians I could appeal to. Where can I go from there? Colonel Wentworth did promise to write if he was able to find anything out for me, but I've had no word yet."

Viscount Tremaine rubbed his forehead in concentration. "It's evident that you must either find a better spokesman or a person of higher rank to whom you could appeal."

"Who?" Edward asked pessimistically. "The Prince is the only person higher up, since the King has little to do with affairs of state anymore. I don't know him, and he's notoriously capricious."

His father was silent a minute, thinking, and then shook his head solemnly. "I've never regretted my country life until now," he said. "I've chosen to stay out of politics and pay the price. I have no influence or friends in high positions. I know it's difficult, but all you can do at this point is wait and see if Colonel Wentworth comes through with something." He shook his head again, deploring his inability to aid his son in a matter that was of such import to him.

Reluctantly, Edward was forced to agree with his father. He could do no more until he had additional information. Perhaps he would hear from Colonel

Wentworth this next week. He said no more about it, and he and his father were soon involved in a discussion of estate matters that lasted until Edward's presence was once again demanded by his guests.

JANE AND FANNY DRESSED carefully Monday afternoon for the picnic, calling on Mrs. Reid with her unerring eye to help them make their choices. She selected a frock of pink spotted cambric for Jane, and added a Venetian bonnet trimmed in yellow ribands and a yellow parasol fringed in pink. For Fanny Mrs. Reid chose a high-waisted white muslin gown trimmed in peach with peach and green accessories.

Edward collected them in a large open carriage and they drove to Bramleigh together. Lady Juliette sat next to Edward, and appeared in excellent looks and spirits. She was charmingly outfitted in a high-necked frock of yellow muslin with long lace-trimmed sleeves and carried a leaf-green parasol fringed in yellow. Edward and Lord Blackwood were both dressed in blue morning coats with buff pantaloons and Hussars. Jamie scorned anything so ordinary as a blue morning coat. He was clad in a coat of the colour known as the parsley mixture, ribbed kerseymere pantaloons and mahogany-coloured top boots.

Chris and Marianne Archer had been invited to join the group, and they were waiting outside with Lord Grandville when the others arrived. They greeted each other merrily, and began the walk to the spot Lord Grandville had selected for the picnic.

Jane looked forward to a pleasurable day, despite the presence of Lady Juliette. The Bramleigh grounds were beautiful. They had been planned by Capability Brown, the popular landscape artist of the mid-eighteenth century, who specialised in making estate grounds look "natural" with hills, streams, ponds, groves, even to sheep grazing.

Lord Grandville had selected a spot by a small stream under a gracefully drooping willow. Servants had already put down rugs and the hampers of food. While the food was being set out, the party found places on the rugs and split into smaller groups. Jane found herself with Lord Blackwood, Fanny sat in a larger group with Marianne, Chris and Jamie, and Edward sat with Lady Juliette. The earl, as a polite host, was attentive to all his guests, but it seemed to Jane he was particularly solicitous of Lady Juliette. Of course, she thought fairly, it could just be that Lady Juliette was demanding a lot of attention.

She looked at Fanny and Edward to see if either of them seemed to notice the care Lord Grandville was lavishing on Lady Juliette, finding her a comfortable spot, filling her plate with delicacies and fanning her when the breezes died. She had had the feeling that Fanny liked the earl, and thought she might be disturbed by his attentions to Lady Juliette, but Fanny seemed content with the attentions of Chris and Jamie. Edward appeared a little stiff, but he was smilingly amiable to Lady Juliette, and his diffidence might have been caused by something else.

Jane gave a shrug and turned her attention back to Lord Blackwood, catching his blue eyes regarding her intently. They exchanged a smile, and quite soon, Jane was too flattered by Lord Blackwood's attendance upon her to think any further of Lady Juliette. When the luncheon was pronounced ready, he filled a plate for her from the food set out, and after filling his own, sat down next to her.

Jane found herself very aware of the way Lord Blackwood's shoulders filled out his coat, and even more so of the muscular thighs outlined by the tight-fitting buff pantaloons revealed when he stretched out beside her. He became aware of her regard and smiled at her lazily. Jane felt her face get hot and sensed he knew just what she was thinking. Perhaps Lord Grandville was right, and Lord Blackwood *was* a rake.

Her appreciation of Lord Blackwood's physique made her feel somehow traitorous, so she looked to find Edward again, just in time to see him place a strawberry into Lady Juliette's inviting mouth. A pain tightened her chest and she quickly turned back to Lord Blackwood.

Lord Blackwood had followed her glance, and now followed Edward's suit, placing a ripe strawberry on Jane's lips. His fingers touched her lips lightly as she bit the strawberry, and she felt a strange pull towards Lord Blackwood. The feeling made her uncomfortable, and she turned away from him, picking up a venison pastry from her plate. She concentrated on eating it, thereby missing Edward's expression of disapproval he had been wearing since the time he had noted Lord Blackwood's action.

After the party finished their leisurely lunch and the servants began repacking the hampers and clearing up, Lord Grandville asked if they would like a tour of Bramleigh. Everyone favoured the suggestion, for Bramleigh was quite the finest house in the district. An opportunity to be shown through it by the owner was not to be missed. Jane had been in the house twice before, for two masquerades prior to the old earl's death, and was curious to see if Lord Grandville had changed anything.

As they went inside the house, Jane considered how while clothes fashions from the 1770s now looked out of style, buildings from the same period seemed quite modern. Bramleigh had been designed by Robert Adam, one of the premier architects of the 1770s. Adam was unusual in that he had not only designed buildings, but also much of the furnishings, even to the carpets.

The large entrance hall was very imposing, with a black-and-white checkered marble floor and large white marble columns around three walls. Six tall windows hung with draperies of blue *gros de Naples* extended the length of the fourth wall. Full-size classical statues were set in niches along the walls between the columns, and several landscapes by Gainsborough hung high above the statues.

Lord Grandville led the party through the hall into the dining room, which was one of Jane's favourite rooms. At each end of the dining room the walls were curved, and the sideboards, also designed by Adam, had been curved to fit. Painted a delicate apple-green, the walls featured sunken panels ornamented with white plasterwork of the same design as that on the ceiling. Jane could see that all the party was impressed with Bramleigh, and she noticed a particularly interested and acquisitive look in Lady Juliette's blue eyes. Edward had better watch out, Jane thought a little unkindly. Three Haverton Parks could fit into one Bramleigh.

A drawing room opened out from the dining room, and the earl led the group there next. The room was done in green, pink and yellow pastels, and was particularly charming. The artist, Angelica Kauffman, had been commissioned to paint a round picture in the centre of the ceiling. The painting was surrounded by plasterwork in a delicate design reflected in the design of the carpet.

Jane was standing aside from the others, admiring a white marble fireplace inlaid with coloured marbles of pink, green and grey, when she noticed something odd. The earl, Fanny, Edward and Lady Juliette were standing together, and Fanny seemed to be pointing out various valuable possessions of Lord Grandville's, calling Lady Juliette's attention to his collection of Sevres and his paintings by Rubens and Poussin. Fanny seemed quite familiar with the house, and Jane wondered when she had been there before, for Fanny had been too young to go to the masquerades Jane had attended. She would have to keep a close eye on Fanny. In her preoccupation with her hurt over Edward, she had neglected her duties as chaperone. A question from Marianne took her thoughts off her sister.

"Why is all the furniture arranged around the walls, Lord Grandville?"

"Odds hoops and panniers," he replied, "there's no room for ladies to walk if one places furniture in the centre of the room."

"Some of the skirts were over six feet wide," Jane elaborated. "It's only since hoops went out of fashion that people began placing furniture in the middle of the room."

Marianne admitted the sense of this, and Lord Grandville led them back into the entrance hall. From there they went up the beautiful curving stairway of wrought iron to the music room. Like the other rooms, the ceiling and walls, here painted in a delicate blue, were decorated with stucco ornament, the designs reflected in the specially woven carpet beneath. The room contained a harpsichord, harp and pianoforte in addition to several chairs and settees. Jane was surprised to see the pianoforte, which was a new addition, and went to look at it closely. It was a beautiful square instrument, of mahogany inlaid with bands of lighter wood. Lord Grandville saw her looking at it and came to join her.

"Are you not cheating, Lord Grandville?" she asked.

Lord Grandville smiled. "No. This is a 1773 pianoforte by Shudi and Broadwood."

Lady Juliette saw Lord Grandville talking to Jane and came to admire the pianoforte, as well. The earl begged her to play a selection, which she did willingly. *I might have known,* Jane thought as she and the others listened, *Lady Juliette is a talented musician on top of all her other accomplishments.* When she finished the Haydn sonata, they effusively complimented her playing. The earl asked if anyone else cared to play, but no one was willing to follow Lady Juliette's expert performance.

The next room on their tour was an unusual circular drawing room decorated in yellow and white. The ceiling was curved, as well, and it gave the room a feeling of great spaciousness. The furniture in the room Jane thought exceptionally beautiful, for it was all pale yellow painted with delicate flowers. The earl explained the furniture had been designed by Kauffman, the same artist who had done the round painting on the ceiling of the ground-floor drawing room. The earl bade them all rest a moment and ordered tea.

"Lord Grandville, are you going to continue the custom of the August masquerade?" Chris asked as they enjoyed their tea.

"Faith, yes. Although my uncle did not specifically request that I do so, by the mass, I believe the neighbourhood would miss it sorely if I did not."

The others agreed wholeheartedly. Lady Juliette, curious, asked about the masquerade.

"M'great-uncle began the tradition to show people of modern times how an entertainment should be conducted. Odds feathers and furbelows, they don't have entertainments like Mrs. Cornely's of Soho Square anymore." He shook his head sadly.

"How did they differ from the ones held today?" Lady Juliette asked, forgetting the earl was not old enough to have attended any.

Lord Grandville thought a moment.

"Imagination. Aye. Today it's all shepherds and shepherdesses. Why, m'uncle once saw Lord Atworth attend a masquerade as Adam—in flesh-coloured tights and a small apron with an embroidered fig leaf."

Marianne Archer and the Hampton sisters blushed at the picture the description conjured up, but Lady Juliette looked intrigued.

"The masquerades are of all things wonderful, Lady Juliette," Chris added enthusiastically. "You will enjoy it excessively."

"I say," suggested Jamie, forgetting to be bored and superior, "why don't you offer a prize to the most imaginative or daring costume?"

"Good idea," Chris seconded.

Lord Grandville, looking at Jamie as though surprised he had any ideas, agreed it was worth considering, although such things were usually not done in the fashionable world.

"Edward," Lady Juliette cried, "why did you not tell me of the masquerade? I brought no costume."

"I am sorry, Lady Juliette, I did not think of it," Edward apologised.

"There is a seamstress in the village who is quite skilled with her needle," Fanny said. "You may get a costume there."

"A village dressmaker would not have the materials I require," Lady Juliette objected. "I would need to go to London, or at least Brighton."

"Odds life," the earl interposed. "Allow me to come to your rescue, Fair Lady. I have a town house in Brighton. We'll get up an excursion."

The earl's idea was quickly endorsed by the Blackwoods and Tremaines, but the Archers and Hamptons hesitated.

"My sister and I have no maid to accompany us," Jane said, "and it wouldn't be proper for us to travel without one."

"That is no problem," Lady Juliette said generously. "My aunt will act as your chaperone as well as mine."

Fanny looked at Jane pleadingly, and Jane capitulated.

"Very well, if Father agrees," she qualified.

"I don't think Mama would allow me to go, and I *have* a maid," Marianne said wistfully.

"I shall go, anyway," Chris said unfeelingly, earning a mutinous look from his sister.

The excursion was set for a week hence, and the day's outing at Bramleigh ended with all except Marianne in high spirits.

THE DAY AFTER THE PICNIC, Lady Juliette wandered absently about the entrance hall at Haverton Park, waiting for her aunt and Lady Tremaine, who were to join her on a drive to Staplefield. How dull Sussex was turning out to be, Lady Juliette thought with a sense of oppression. No routs, assemblies, opera or theatre, only country balls and dinners. And as for the company! Lady Tremaine was as prosy as Edward had turned out to be, and the Hampton sisters were hopelessly provincial. She was quite bored out of all patience.

Well, she thought, yawning delicately, as soon as she could bring Edward to the point she would return to London. Or perhaps she should think of transferring her affections to Lord Grandville—he appeared to be interested in her.

She stopped in front of the gilt-framed mirror to adjust the tilt of her gypsy hat and tie the ribands in a more flattering bow. As she adjusted the hat, she noticed some letters lying on a salver on the table beneath the mirror. The top letter caught her eye, and glancing about quickly to see if anyone was looking, she picked it up. From Colonel Wentworth. Wasn't that the man Edward had been asking to look into the matter of Sir John? Impulsively she stuck the letter into the bosom of her gown and went back up to her bedchamber, passing Dawkins at the base of the stairs.

Safe in her room, she dismissed Parkins and took out the letter, fingering it thoughtfully. She wondered what it said. Edward had gone to London to see Colonel

Wentworth before. What if he was being asked to do so again? If he were to absent himself from Sussex for a long period of time, she would be forced to leave herself. It would appear odd for her to remain if the person who had invited her was no longer in residence. Or if she did remain, who knew how long it would be before Edward returned? She could not bear to remain in Sussex too long.

She made her decision, and squashing a momentary feeling of guilt, opened the letter and scanned it quickly. Colonel Wentworth *did* want Edward to come to London, to see the brother of Sir John Moore. She folded the letter up slowly. No, it would not do if Edward were to read the letter. Much as she disliked Sussex, she couldn't afford to leave now, not with the interest Lord Grandville was beginning to show in her. She slipped the letter under the lining of her jewel box and went back downstairs to wait for her aunt and Lady Tremaine.

CHAPTER EIGHT

THAT WEDNESDAY EVENING, the Archers held one of the country dinners Lady Juliette so despised. The company at the dinner was the same as that which had been at the Tremaines' ball. Except when one family or another had guests, the company was always the same in country society, but it did not lessen their enjoyment of the entertainments.

Jane had been looking forward to the dinner, hoping to talk to Lord Blackwood. Therefore, she was rather disappointed to be escorted into dinner by Christopher Archer and be placed between him and her father. She looked wistfully down the table to where Lord Blackwood and Edward were seated, and then scolded herself for being uncharitable. Christopher might be an aspiring dandy such as Jamie, with his high shirt points and outrageously tight and brightly coloured coats and pantaloons, but he was a nice young man. As the vegetable soup was taken away and the dishes of the second remove placed on the table, she turned to Chris with a compliment on his coat, and his face pinked with pleasure.

"Thank you, Miss Hampton. Must say, you're in excellent looks yourself this evening. Very becoming gown," he said, viewing her with appreciation. She was wearing a new gown she had ordered from the village dressmaker after Lady Juliette had arrived in Sussex with her fashionable wardrobe. It had short white puff sleeves over tight pink undersleeves and a high-waisted skirt belted with pink satin riband.

Chris helped himself to some of the fried chicken breasts in the dish before him and offered them to Jane. As she took one and passed the dish to her father, it occurred to Jane to wonder if there would be a repeat of the conversation on the Peninsular War. She hoped for Captain Tremaine's sake there would not be. Fortunately the subject did not come up, and the dinner passed pleasantly.

The arrival of coffee indicated the end of the meal, and time for the women to leave the men to their port and cigars. Lady Archer signalled the ladies to follow her into the drawing room where they would visit until the gentlemen rejoined them.

Jane seated herself on a Sheraton-style settee, where she was joined by the vicar's wife, Mrs. Fairchild, and Mrs. Shirley, the squire's lady. Fanny and Marianne took side chairs next to each other, and Lady Martin settled into the most comfortable-looking armchair. Jane noticed that Lady Juliette sat a little apart from the rest of the company, making no attempt to join in conversation with any of the woman. Not for the first time, it occurred to Jane that Lady Juliette rarely exhibited her charm of manner when there were no gentlemen present. At the moment she was making no effort whatsoever to disguise her boredom with the company as she looked restlessly about the room. Lady Archer must have noticed Lady Juliette's *ennui*, for she suggested to Marianne that she play a selection on the spinet to entertain the guests.

Marianne obediently left Fanny to go to the instrument, a pretty spinet of satinwood veneer, and played a light country air, accompanying herself in a clear if weak voice. Fanny joined her at the piano and added her soft soprano to Marianne's, and Jane went to add her deeper contralto. Lady Juliette did not join the group about the spinet, however, and after a few songs Lady Archer tried another tack with her difficult guest.

"Lady Juliette, would you do us the favour of playing a selection? My son Chris tells me you are a talented performer."

"Of course, I should be pleased to, Lady Archer," Lady Juliette replied, thus appealed to directly for her participation in the entertainment. She took Marianne's place at the spinet, spreading her silken skirts gracefully about the stool.

"My niece is quite talented," Lady Martin proclaimed in loud tones as Lady Juliette riffled through the music Marianne offered her. "You will be quite edified by her performance, although, of course, she requires a proper pianoforte to do her playing justice," she finished, looking at the Archers' modest instrument with disdain.

Lady Juliette made her selection and launched into a difficult sonata by Mozart. Much as Jane disliked

Lady Juliette, she was forced to appreciate her undeniable talent. It cast Marianne's performance quite into the shade. Yet as Jane listened to the cascade of notes rippling through the room, she wondered if that had not been Lady Juliette's purpose. She had intentionally chosen a piece that would demonstrate the superiority of her accomplishments to the rest of the company. Jane tried to dismiss the ungenerous thought and enjoy the music, but the suspicion remained.

While Lady Juliette was still playing, the gentlemen rejoined the ladies, and, if possible, Lady Juliette's playing became even more brilliant. Lord Grandville and Captain Tremaine stood beside the spinet, watching Lady Juliette's fingers as they flew unerringly over the keys. At the end of the sonata the company applauded Lady Juliette enthusiastically. She smiled graciously and inclined her head in recognition of the applause. Lord Grandville requested she honour them with another selection, and Lady Juliette complied, choosing a short but technically difficult piece by Bach.

As Jane watched Lady Juliette, to whom the music was familiar enough that she was able to smile up at the gentlemen as she played, she mused how gullible men appeared to be. They would never see that her charm was a veneer, or better, a mask, put on and off at will. They were quite taken in by her pretty face and the pretty manners Lady Juliette could display when she chose, Jane thought resignedly.

Lady Juliette finished her second selection to more generous applause, and would not allow herself to be talked into a third. She rose from the stool with a smile, and was escorted to a chair by Lord Grandville and Captain Tremaine.

"Come, what say we have a rubber of whist?" Baron Archer suggested before his wife could ask another guest to perform on the spinet. "Let us leave the youngsters to themselves," he added with a wink toward Fanny and Chris.

Jane smiled at Baron Archer's obvious ploy. The baron was an inveterate card player, and evenings at his home inevitably ended in a game. She had noticed the card tables had already been set up in the smaller drawing room adjoining the one they were in, and she could see the servants moving about, lighting the candles at the corners of the card tables.

The older guests got up and went into the adjoining room, obediently following their host's suggestion. Jane went to stand in the doorway a moment to see if her presence would be needed to make up a table, but seeing that it was not, returned to her place on the settee. She did not see her father in either room, and had no doubt he was to be found in the baron's rather sparsely furnished library.

"I say, why don't we try a few dances?" Chris suggested to the company remaining in the larger drawing room.

There was general agreement, and without bothering to ring for servants, the men moved the furniture to the walls and rolled up the carpets. Marianne good-naturedly volunteered to play, and struck up a boulanger. Jane watched wistfully as Captain Tremaine led Lady Juliette onto the floor. She was not left alone though, for Lord Blackwood came up to her.

"Will you do me the honour of granting me your hand for this dance?" he asked with exaggerated formality.

"It would be a pleasure, Lord Blackwood," Jane replied with a curtsy, and they joined the others on the small floor. Lord Blackwood was an excellent dancer, and Jane soon lost the hint of sadness she had felt upon seeing Captain Tremaine choose Lady Juliette as his first partner.

After three dances, Lady Juliette graciously offered to take Marianne's place so she could have a chance to dance, too, and before long the whole company was hot and flushed with their exertions. Lady Juliette stopped playing, and Chris opened the doors to the gardens. Cool breezes blew temptingly, and there was a general exodus to the garden.

Jane felt another twinge of envy when she saw Captain Tremaine escort Lady Juliette outside, but Lord Blackwood was again at Jane's side, his flattering attention erasing her momentary hurt. They wandered down a gravel path to a bench near some fragrant pinks where they sat down to enjoy the breeze and the perfume of the flowers. Lord Blackwood seemed very relaxed, and he smiled at Jane contentedly.

"My experience of country life here in Sussex is tempting me to settle in the district, Miss Hampton," he confessed.

Jane laughed. "It may seem peaceful and pleasurable to you for the moment, but I feel very sure you would soon miss the excitement of the city and become bored."

"I think it might depend upon the company I kept," Lord Blackwood replied with a meaningful look at Jane. "Do you ever become bored and long for the excitement of a new way of life?"

"No, but I am content with country pastimes because I have never known anything else. I do not think my excursions to Bath would count."

"I suppose you are correct," Lord Blackwood admitted, and began to question Jane about her life.

Jane answered Lord Blackwood unreservedly, feeling quite comfortable with him. She told him of her quiet upbringing as a vicar's daughter, and when she had finished, was bold enough to ask him to reciprocate.

"Now it's your turn, sir," she teased.

"I fear my life has not been as edifying as yours," Lord Blackwood replied. "My father was a gambler, and although my mother tried her best to make ends meet, she did not succeed. We were never more than a step away from debtor's prison. When I became old enough my father taught me to play at cards, and as I had rather more luck than he, the family came to depend on my winnings." Lord Blackwood went on to describe his family's hand-to-mouth existence, culminating in the flight of his father to the Continent after a duel.

Jane listened sympathetically, his confidences causing her to warm to him. She thought it also helped explain Lady Juliette's apparent determination to marry a man of wealth. Yet, she thought, it still did not excuse the unkindness she had so often observed in Lady Juliette. Lord Blackwood grew up under the same conditions, after all, and *he* was not unkind.

Lord Blackwood finished his recital, and they lapsed into silence, sharing the peace of the evening, listening to a nightingale and breathing in the sweet evening perfume of the Hesperis as it mingled with the spicy fragrance of the pinks. Jane was staring into the distance looking at nothing in particular and thinking of Lord Blackwood's unhappy life when she felt a light touch on her cheek. She turned to face Lord Blackwood, and he bent his face to hers, kissing her softly on her lips. Unless she counted the curate at her father's former parish near Bath, this was Jane's first kiss. And as she experienced Lord Blackwood's expert kiss, she decided the curate's definitely did *not* count. The curate's kiss had not stirred her like this.

Lord Blackwood's lips became more demanding as Jane did not resist him, his tongue forcing her lips open and invading her mouth, and his arms went about her shoulders to hold her close. Jane was startled but not repulsed, and strange new feelings ran down her spine clear to her feet. She leaned into his kiss, her arms going about him involuntarily. She was beginning to feel oddly light-headed when she heard a crunch of gravel.

At the sound of the footstep, she quickly pulled away, fearful of being seen. Lord Blackwood let her go without protest, but his eyes glowed strangely, and Jane looked away uncomfortably. Although they did not see anyone, whomever they had heard evidently having taken another path had broken the mood. Jane stood up rather shakily, wanting to escape Lord Blackwood and return to the safety of the others. Lord Blackwood stood up as well and, without speaking, accompanied her back inside.

EDWARD STARTED TO WALK back to the house, then changed his mind and went down the gravel path to a bench near a Greek-style statue. He had several things he wished to think over privately. The kiss he had interrupted between Jane and Lord Blackwood had disturbed him. Jane was so innocent, unused to the ways of men such as Adrian Blackwood. Although he liked Lady Juliette's brother, for he was very good company, Edward was aware of his reputation and quite sure it was deserved. He frowned as he remembered the strawberry Adrian had placed between Jane's lips on the picnic, forgetting he had done the same with Lady Juliette.

Edward sighed. He would have to warn Jane, and he was not quite sure how to do so. But he could not allow Jane to fall in love with a rake and have her heart broken or her reputation ruined.

He stood up and scuffed at the statue with his top boots, ruining the shine Ames had laboured to put on them. The summer was not turning out to be as he had planned. Lady Juliette did not seem the same here in Sussex, and he was disappointed with the reception she had been given. Although his parents were impeccably hospitable, their welcome had somehow lacked warmth. Jamie was courteous when he spoke to her, but he ignored her when he could, a state of affairs that was mutual, he admitted fairly. Jane, whom he had envisaged becoming fast friends with Lady Juliette, was polite but distant. Not that he could blame her; Lady Martin was quite unkind to both Jane and Fanny, and Lady Juliette had done nothing to moderate her behaviour.

Edward was a little surprised at Lady Juliette's failure to stop her aunt from making unkind comments to Jane and Fanny. Although he did not like to admit it, Lady Juliette's conduct did not seem as charming as it had in London. For instance, there was her churlishness at dinner tonight. She had been placed between himself and Jamie, and since his attention had been claimed by the vicar's wife, Mrs. Fairchild, Jamie had tried to be civil and converse with Lady Juliette. But she had rudely ignored his efforts, sitting in morose silence until Lord Grandville had engaged her in conversation. He thought of the contrast this made with Jane, who had good-naturedly conversed with that young sprig of fashion she had been placed next to.

He thought of Lady Juliette and Lord Grandville. The charming manners she had exhibited towards himself in London she now exhibited whenever the earl was about. Her flirting bothered him somewhat, and he wondered about the earl's motives. Were his gallantries part of that absurd act he put on in her presence, or was there something more serious underlying them? Edward began to wish he had never met the Blackwoods; they were cutting up his peace so. He gave the statue a final kick and wandered back to the house.

THAT EVENING for the first time, as she lay in bed with the fragrant night air coming through the open window, Jane thought seriously of Lord Blackwood and what his intentions towards her might be. She was realistic enough to know that as the daughter of a country clergyman, with no great beauty or fortune, she was unlikely to be the object of his serious intentions. Too, Fanny had told her the earl had hinted that Lord Blackwood was something of a rake. Jane had dreamed that a country gentleman such as Edward might care for her. After all, his sister was married to a simple squire herself. But if Edward could not love her, it was highly unlikely that a man such as Lord Blackwood would. He was probably just amusing himself with her. But even as she knew that, his attentions were flattering. At least one man found her attractive.

AS JANE LAY IN HER BED assessing her situation with the interesting Lord Blackwood, he was knocking on the door of his sister's dressing room. The lord had decided that sibling loyalty behooved him to warn his sister that she was in danger of losing her quarry.

Lady Juliette sat on a stool before her dressing table, her maid vigorously brushing her glossy black hair. Adrian looked at the maid meaningfully.

"You may go, Parkins," Juliette said, and turned to her brother as the maid left the room, closing the door behind her. Adrian took a delicate Hepplewhite chair, straddled it, and resting his elbows on the top, he gazed at his sister thoughtfully.

"Tell me, sister, are you going for a bigger fish?"

"And if I am?" Lady Juliette asked, turning her back to him and reviewing herself in the glass with satisfaction.

"Be careful. At the risk of talking in clichés, I should remind you a bird in the hand is worth two in the bush."

Lady Juliette tapped her fingers impatiently on the dressing table.

"Edward has not made an offer yet. Let him compete for my attentions. A woman who is too easy to capture is not worth the hunt."

Adrian knew that was true of many men, but was not sure it applied to Edward. He said as much to his sister.

Lady Juliette shook her head impatiently. "Don't criticise my tactics. What about you? What are you doing setting up a flirtation with the Hampton girl? Don't ruin my chances by making Edward angry. He is protective of the family for some reason. Perhaps because the younger girl is betrothed to his ridiculous popinjay of a brother, or so I have heard, although they don't behave as if they are engaged."

Adrian shrugged. "There aren't any country heiresses in the district. I must amuse myself somehow, and Miss Hampton seems the very thing."

"Just see that your amusements don't interfere with my plans. Now if you've said what you came to say, you may leave. Have Parkins come back in as you go."

Adrian stood and sauntered out, pausing at the door of Lady Juliette's bedchamber to summon Parkins to attend to her mistress again. He had warned his sister; more than that he could not do. Or would not, he admitted to himself. He admired his sister and had an affection for her, but he also got enormous pleasure out of seeing her machinations fail.

THE NEXT MORNING, for a change, Jane did not attempt to cancel riding out with the guests at Haverton Park. She was curious to see Lord Blackwood again, and wondered if she would feel differently towards him after the kiss of the night before.

Lord Blackwood rode beside her as they started out, talking to her in the same easy manner, but his eyes seemed to hold a special message. The familiarity made her feel slightly uncomfortable, and she was relieved when he galloped off with the majority of the party, leaving her with Edward.

Edward trotted beside her silently for a moment, seeming rather distracted, and then asked her to stop.

Jane looked at him in surprise but did as he requested. He directed Ariel to a fence, tethered him and dismounted, and then helped her to dismount, as well. Jane leaned against the fence, with Edward next to her, a look of uncertainty on his face. She waited for him to say what was on his mind.

"I felt I must speak to you about the attentions you have been receiving from Lord Blackwood," he began a little hesitantly. "You are not accustomed to society and not acquainted with his type. Although I know his attentions must be flattering, don't read too much into them."

As Edward spoke, Jane began to feel angry. Did he think that because he did not find her attractive as a woman, no other man could? How dared he presume to lecture her on her behaviour!

"I may not be accustomed to the rarefied heights of society you are, Captain Tremaine, but that does not mean I am no judge of character," she said when he finished, barely containing her temper.

"Now I have made you angry," he said. He was making a mull of things. He must try again. "I speak to you as a brother might, had you one. Lord Blackwood has an unsavoury reputation as far as women are concerned."

Edward was only saying the same things that Jane had said to herself the night before, but she did not like hearing them from him.

"What right do you have to condemn my conduct? You forget I have a father. If there is anything amiss with my conduct *he* will speak to me."

Now Edward also began to lose his temper and was moved to speak unguardedly.

"Perhaps your father did not witness the kiss in the shrubbery last night that I did. Your reputation could have been ruined had anyone other than myself seen you with Lord Blackwood in such a compromising position."

Jane was now thoroughly angry. "So that was you whose foot I heard upon the gravel, spying upon me. When does a single kiss ruin a reputation? Do you mean to tell me that you have never kissed Lady Juliette?" The picture this conjured up in her mind made her angrier than ever. "Do you feel it is impossible for a man to find me attractive, Captain Tremaine?"

"No!" Edward brushed his hair back in the familiar gesture that indicated frustration. "But a kiss may go further—"

"Are you telling me you have so little faith in my character that I would allow Lord Blackwood to seduce me?" Jane demanded. She knew the conversation was now bordering on the improper, but she was too angry to care.

"That is *not* what I mean..." Edward faltered as he realised that was exactly what he meant. How could he explain to an innocent young girl—and that's what Jane was, even if she was four-and-twenty—how events could happen almost without one's being aware? He knew he had no right to censure Jane's conduct, but he had become accustomed to thinking of her as his sister and had felt he ought to protect her and look out for her best interests.

When Edward seemed to have no more to say, Jane climbed on the fence and used it to remount her horse before he could move to help her. Without waiting for him, Jane rode off to find the rest of the party. Edward followed her more slowly, thinking how to repair his blunder. When he caught up with the others he wondered if he had done more harm than good as he noticed Jane in animated conversation with Lord Blackwood. He might have driven her right into his arms.

CHAPTER NINE

"EDWARD, AREN'T YOU GOING with us to Staplefield this morning? You will have to make haste with your breakfast if you are."

Friday morning, Lady Juliette smiled enchantingly at Edward over her empty plate. She was in a cheerful mood, knowing she was in her best looks wearing a multicoloured sprigged muslin gown with a low rounded neckline filled in with a kerchief.

Edward looked up from his full plate and glanced around the table. Everyone had finished eating but him.

"I hope you will excuse me today, Lady Juliette," he said, laying his fork down. "I must forgo the pleasure of your company this morning to take care of some business affairs."

"What can be so important that it can't wait until this afternoon?"

Edward smiled at her persistence. "I am afraid I must not allow you to persuade me this morning, Lady Juliette. Your company is so tempting that I have neglected my correspondence and other affairs shockingly since you have been here."

The compliment did little to mollify Lady Juliette. She regarded Edward closely. His interest in her was beginning to wane—it was definitely not as strong as it once had been if she could not persuade him to spend the morning with her instead of his business. Feeling it only fair, she would redouble her efforts to engage Edward's interest before turning her sights on the earl. Lucky she had taken the letter from Colonel Wentworth. To have had to leave Sussex at this juncture would have been fatal to her plans.

"Well, stay if you wish. I am going," she said aloud. She turned to Edward's brother. "You will accompany us, won't you, Jamie? My aunt and I need someone to help us with our parcels."

"Glad to be of assistance, Lady Juliette," Jamie agreed, albeit not very willingly. The idea of a morning playing footman was not the most appealing.

Lord Blackwood smiled at Jamie knowingly, and Lady Martin looked offended at the reluctance of their hosts to accompany them wherever they might wish to go.

"I'm sure we don't wish to put you out," she said frostily, her habitually severe expression exacerbated by a frown.

Jamie forced more enthusiasm into his voice. "Not at all. Delighted to be of service," he said, looking at Edward with an expression that told his brother he thought he owed him a favour.

Slightly more satisfied, Lady Martin rose majestically from the table and left the room, followed by her niece, nephew and Jamie.

Edward remained at the table after the others left, the kidneys on his plate congealing in their gravy. He *had* neglected all his other affairs since bringing the Blackwoods to Haverton Park. Lady Juliette was not used to the slow pace of country life, but despite his best efforts to keep her amused, she was becoming bored with country activities, he could see.

He wondered if Juliette would be satisfied with the life he had to offer her. He cared little for society; she thrived on it. He saw how she basked in the admiration of the earl and wondered about the relationship developing between Lady Juliette and Lord Grandville. Although Lord Grandville continued to address her in that ridiculously outmoded style of expression, Lady Juliette did not seem to object. Perhaps Lord Grandville's gallantries to her were more sincere than he had at first thought?

He wished he had someone to talk to about Lady Juliette. He missed the morning visits he had become accustomed to with Jane before he had gone to London. Since the Blackwoods had come, they had of necessity ended. He could not leave his guests every morning to visit somewhere else.

He went to the sideboard and lifted the covers off the dishes one by one. Somehow nothing looked very tempting this morning. He returned to his place at the table to finish a cup of coffee.

He remembered that Jane probably wouldn't talk to him in any event, not after their altercation over Lord Blackwood.

"Miss Hampton has asked to speak with you. I have put her in the Rose Drawing Room," Dawkins announced, as if Edward's thoughts had conjured up her actual presence.

"Thank you, Dawkins. I will join her immediately," Edward replied. He wondered what had brought Jane to Haverton Park. He certainly hadn't expected her to seek his company so soon after their falling-out.

Jane sat on the gracefully curved window seat in the drawing room, admiring the flowers in Lady Tremaine's garden. She was wearing the pink print frock he had first seen her in, and a wide-brimmed bonnet.

"Good morning, Jane," he said to announce his presence. "What brings me the pleasure of your company this morning?"

"I have this for you," she explained, walking forward and holding out a thick letter. "I hope you will not think it presumptuous of me to have had my father write on your behalf."

Mystified, Edward took the letter and perused it, his face lighting as he began to comprehend. "Why, this is of all things wonderful, Jane. Colonel Fisher writes that he has also been concerned about the damaging things being said of Sir John. He gives me the direction of someone who may be able to help—Sir Howard

Douglas—and includes a letter of introduction. He suggests that I may be able to arrange to see him next week in Brighton."

At the pleasure on his face, Jane was glad she had got over her pique long enough to bring him the letter. Her father had received it yesterday, but at the time she had still been so angry that she had been tempted not to deliver it at all.

"I can't thank you enough," Edward continued, inviting Jane to sit whereupon he seated himself in a chair next to her. "I had reached an impasse. Colonel Wentworth never wrote as he had promised, and I had no other leads. Where did you hear of Colonel Fisher and his interest in Sir John?"

Jane explained about the original letter from the Bishop of Salisbury.

"I didn't want to tell you and get your hopes up if it were to come to nothing," she added.

Edward was greatly touched by her thoughtfulness. He looked at her, sitting on the heart-shaped chair, a smile of pleasure bringing the elusive dimple to her cheek, and had a sudden urge to place a kiss upon the dimple. He quickly suppressed the urge.

"Jane," he was moved to say, wanting their previous relationship to be restored, "will you please forgive my speaking to you yesterday about Lord Blackwood? You were right, of course—it is none of my affair."

"I have already forgiven you," she replied, happy to be in charity with Edward once more. "I know you have my best interests at heart. You needn't worry about me, though. I know Lord Blackwood is a rake, and I am in no danger of losing my heart to him."

Edward reflected that it wasn't only her heart he was concerned about, but said nothing, not wanting to be in her bad graces again.

Dawkins came to the door with a message that they were to join Lady Tremaine and Fanny in the Green Drawing Room, and they went downstairs together, in accord with each other once more.

"I have been trying to persuade Fanny to accept an invitation to join us for lunch," Lady Tremaine said to Jane. "The Blackwoods have gone to Staplefield for the morning, but they will return before long. I should be glad of your company to help amuse them."

Jane rather doubted their company was very amusing to Lady Juliette but agreed to stay. They spent the time waiting for the return of the others conversing pleasantly.

The party to Staplefield returned about one o'clock, enlarged by the presence of the earl, whom they had met at a shop in Staplefield. He was invited to stay to lunch also, and Dawkins was told to have another place laid at the table. Lord Tremaine came down from his study, and they all went in to dine.

"What could we do this afternoon?" Lady Juliette asked no one in particular as she picked at an apricot tart on her plate.

Fanny spoke up. "What about a berry-picking expedition? The brambles are ripe."

Jane regarded her sister in surprise. A country pastime such as berry-picking would be the last thing to appeal to a woman like Lady Juliette. She intercepted an odd look that passed between the earl and Fanny.

"*Berry* picking," Lady Juliette said, a scornful tone in her voice.

"Odds fruits and prickles, a splendid idea, Miss Fanny," Lord Grandville approved. He addressed Lady Juliette. "Berry picking is a famous country pastime. By the mass, your visit to Sussex would not be complete without a berry-picking expedition."

Jane almost laughed to see how Lady Juliette's reluctance turned to enthusiasm at the earl's endorsement. The outing was set for three o'clock that afternoon, and a note was sent to the Archer children to ask them to join. Jane and Fanny went home as soon as the luncheon was over to prepare for the expedition.

LATER THAT AFTERNOON the sisters returned to Haverton Park wearing old long-sleeved dresses of stout cotton, their heads covered with deep-brimmed bonnets and carrying milk pails for their share of the berries. The men were appropriately clad in buckskins and old coats, but Jane looked at Lady Juliette's clothes doubtfully. She was wearing a light muslin dress that would be torn easily by the thorns. She had to admit Lady Juliette did look charming, though, in the fragile fabric decorated with ribands and lace.

Lady Juliette looked at the Hamptons' clothes just as dubiously. "How charming," she exclaimed. "Milkmaids."

Jane flushed, but felt better when Marianne Archer arrived clad similarly.

Edward had located some brambles that were ripe a little way behind Haverton Park, and they set out in high spirits.

"A guinea to the first one to fill his pail," Chris called, and the party began picking enthusiastically.

Fanny took charge of Lady Juliette, showing her which berries to pick and leading her to a spot she claimed had lots of ripe ones.

Jane could not like the place Fanny had selected for Lady Juliette. The bushes were very thick, and Lady Juliette's clothes were likely to get caught in the bushes, but she made no comment. Sure enough, in a short time there was a cry from Lady Juliette; her skirts had become stuck fast in the brambles. Lord Grandville, Jane, Edward and Fanny went immediately to her aid, but they were unable to free her without tearing her dress.

"You knew I would stick in the brambles here," Lady Juliette accused Fanny, her face crimson with anger. "You little jade! My dress is ruined beyond repair," she spat venomously.

Jane rather suspected Lady Juliette's accusation was correct, and said nothing in Fanny's defence. Edward looked disapprovingly at both Fanny and Lady

Juliette. The others pretended not to notice the altercation, returning to their berry picking.

Lady Juliette assessed the torn and stained ruin of her dress and her anger got the better of her. Thinking she was unobserved, she swung her pail wildly at Fanny, who stepped backwards to avoid it and fell into the brambles.

Serves Fanny right, Jane thought, *for being so unkind*. But when she went to pull her sister out of the bushes she found that Fanny had sustained a deep cut on her forearm and was bleeding profusely. She called for aid, and Chris ran to the stream to wet a cloth, sacrificing his cravat for that purpose. Edward and Lord Grandville led Fanny to the shade of a tree and persuaded her to lie down. Her arm was bound securely, and within a few minutes Fanny declared she was feeling fine and returned to picking berries.

Lady Juliette, furious at the attention Fanny was getting and the disapproving glances she had received, insisted Edward take her home. Reluctantly Edward agreed, looking back wistfully at the party, who, spirits restored after the mishap, were once again competing to see who would fill a pail first.

THE REMAINDER OF THE PARTY returned to Haverton Park about five, laughing and covered with berry stains, congratulating Marianne, who had won the guinea. They joined Lady Tremaine, Lady Martin, Lady Juliette and Edward in the Green Drawing Room. Lady Juliette had changed into a fresh gown and appeared cool and beautiful. Lady Tremaine invited them all to stay for dinner, but Lord Grandville and the Archers had to refuse because of prior commitments. Fanny and Jane protested that they could not remain in their untidy clothes, and there was no time to go home and change.

"That's no problem," Lady Tremaine said. "Jane and I are of a size, and she may borrow a gown from me." She looked at Lady Juliette, who could not fail to offer one of hers to Fanny without looking churlish, since they were both of slender build.

"I suppose I can find you something you could wear, Miss Fanny," she said rather ungraciously, rising to lead Fanny upstairs to her dressing room.

The lady looked through her wardrobe impatiently. She spied a fawn-coloured silk trimmed in red that had never flattered her and thrust it at Fanny.

"Here, this should fit. Parkins will help you dress," she said with a nod to the abigail, and proceeded to go back downstairs.

Fanny suspected why Lady Juliette chose that particular gown and was relieved when it proved to be quite attractive on her. She washed her face and hands, and after fixing her hair, started back downstairs. Near the landing, she was waylaid by Jamie.

"I say, Fan, will you come in the library a moment? I wish to speak to you."

Reluctantly Fanny agreed. She followed him to the library, an impressive room filled with volumes bound in leather and stamped with the Tremaine crest. She sa in a comfortable chair by the window and waited for Jamie to speak.

"Look here, Fan, why won't you reinstate our betrothal?" he asked, sitting down next to her, his expression full of entreaty.

"I told you why before," she replied, steadily. She felt a moment's regret as she looked at the handsome young man she had once loved. His red-gold hair glinted in the afternoon sunlight that filtered into the room, and his hazel eyes regarded her appealingly. When she did not relent, he jumped up and began pacing back and forth angrily.

"I do not accept your reason. I know the real one and you may as well give it up. The earl is not interested in you. He prefers Lady Juliette."

"Everyone must admire Lady Juliette's beauty," Fanny said calmly. "Jamie, can't you see that we should make each other unhappy?"

"I don't see that," Jamie objected, coming to sit by her again. "You thought we should make each other happy before. How has it changed?"

"It changed when my beauty changed," Fanny said, rising. There was no point in discussing it with Jamie; he wouldn't listen.

As she walked past him towards the door, Jamie grabbed her by the arm and tried to kiss her, hoping that would rekindle her feelings, but she pushed him away strongly.

"Stop that, James Tremaine. I want this betrothal ended. If you won't, I will," she stormed angrily, slamming the heavy door behind her as she left the room.

DURING DINNER Edward watched the others enjoying themselves and wished he were seated next to Jane or Fanny and not Lady Juliette. Lady Juliette was still in a bad mood from the day's happenings and said little, looking sullenly at Fanny. Edward followed her glance. He recognised the fawn-coloured silk as one that was not flattering to Lady Juliette, and smiled. He knew she had chosen it purposely and was glad her plan had backfired.

His eyes went to Jane, who was looking especially fine in a striped silk gown of his mother's. He remembered he had not told his father of the letter to the Bishop of Salisbury Mr. Hampton had written at Jane's urging, or of the promising letter he had received from Colonel Fisher as a result. As soon as there was a break in the conversation, he rectified the omission.

"How thoughtful of you, Miss Hampton," Viscount Tremaine said gratefully. "The situation has been very disturbing to Edward. I appreciate what you've done."

Lady Tremaine added her thanks, but Lady Juliette and Lady Martin did not look impressed.

"One must appreciate the thought, but ladies should not involve themselves in matters of war and politics," Lady Martin admonished. "Of course, in one of your background it may be forgiven," she added condescendingly.

Jane only smiled at Lady Martin's statement. Tonight the woman's supercilious attitude had no power to wound her.

Lady Juliette, angry at having been overshadowed first by Fanny and now by Jane, still felt a twinge of guilt at the thought of the letter resting in her jewellery box. Oh, well, thanks to Miss Hampton's interference, Edward would be able to resolve his problem, and without leaving Sussex. She wondered why it mattered so much to him, anyway.

CHAPTER TEN

TO JANE AND FANNY'S disgust, when the carriage came to collect them Monday for the excursion to Brighton, they found that they were to travel in a carriage with Lady Martin, while Edward, Juliette and her maid rode in another. The earl, Jamie and Lord Blackwood rode horseback.

Lady Martin proved to be a very dampening presence, indicating by her expression that she did not care to be travelling with the sisters. She sat unsmilingly and made several acidulous comments about young women who did not have a maid. Jane and Fanny responded mildly and tried to converse between themselves, but soon gave up and passed the time looking out the windows at the countryside. Lord Blackwood, who rode alongside the carriage, looked in and gave Jane a commiserating smile. The only bright spots in the long day's journey were the stops at posting inns to change horses. There at least they had a few moments to escape Lady Martin and converse with the others. By the time they arrived in Brighton late that evening they were more than ready to relax in the congenial atmosphere of Lord Grandville's town house.

Lord Grandville's residence in Brighton was a very large modern town house. The staff had been notified of their impending arrival and their chambers were ready. Jane and Fanny were shown to adjoining rooms on the first floor. They were furnished identically in painted Sheraton-style furniture, but Jane's chamber was decorated in shades of rose and Fanny's in blue.

As they admired their accommodations, a young maid appeared to offer her services during their stay. With her help they removed the stains of travel and dressed for dinner. It was quite a luxury for them to have someone to style their hair and help them dress. Mrs. Reid only did so on special occasions. Jane reflected that it would be very easy to become accustomed to having such service. She looked at her image in the cheval glass with satisfaction. The maid had done her hair in a new style, with curls dangling from a knot on the top, and she thought it was very becoming.

When the maid pronounced herself satisfied with their appearance, the sisters went down to the ground floor drawing room to wait for dinner to be announced. Lady Juliette and her aunt were not yet down, but the gentlemen had already gathered there. Jane thought at first there was a strange man in the room, but then realised the modishly clad young man with dark brown hair in a Brutus crop was the earl. The close-fitting current fashions outlined a trim and muscular form. She looked at Fanny in surprise, and then remembered the terms of the will were not in effect at Brighton.

Lady Juliette and her aunt came in shortly after, and also looked at the earl in surprise.

"I did not recognise you for a moment, Lord Grandville," Lady Juliette said, admiring his fashionably clad form.

"I was pleased to find my valet still remembered how to tie a current cravat," Lord Grandville replied, speaking to her for the first time without using phrases in vogue in the 1770s. He looked at Lady Juliette with evidently equal appreciation, admiring the picture she presented in her gown of white sarcenet trimmed in Spanish-style ornament.

"Don't you get weary of wearing those old-fashioned clothes?" Lady Juliette dared to ask. "Did you never think of contesting your uncle's will?"

Shocked at Lady Juliette's presumption in asking such a personal question, Jane ventured to look at Lord Grandville. However, he seemed to take no offence, although the smile on his lips did not reach his eyes.

"No, Lady Juliette. The money was my great-uncle's. I had no part in amassing it, and little expectation of inheriting. I am grateful to him and feel the least I can do is to honour his wishes to the fullest of my ability. It is no hardship to me, particularly when the terms are only in effect when I am in residence at Bramleigh. In fact, I find I have quite enjoyed my introduction into the customs of the last century."

Sensing the earl's disapproval of her enquiry, Lady Juliette subsided and her aunt changed the subject with an admonitory look at her niece.

The butler announced dinner, and Lord Blackwood escorted Jane into the dining room, seating her with care at the gleaming mahogany table.

"You look very charmingly, Miss Hampton," he complimented her. "I trust you did not find the journey too tedious?" he added with a meaningful glance at his aunt.

Jane was never sure how to reply to Lord Blackwood's ironical comments, and contented herself with a smile and slight shake of her head. He smiled back and they applied themselves to the savoury-smelling dishes being placed upon the table.

Jane ate her dinner with appreciation, for Mrs. Reid's cooking, while good, was simple. She had never had anything like salad of pike fillets with oysters, and whitefish with herb sauce. It was just as well, she thought, or she would soon be as fat as butter.

Lord Grandville had asked Lady Martin to function as his hostess, and after the fruit she led the women into the drawing room while the men stayed at the table for their port. They did not linger over their port long but soon joined the women to make plans for the next day. Since Jane and Fanny had never been to Brighton, it was decided they would spend the next day exploring the town for the sisters' benefit. Lady Juliette did not look too happy about delaying her shopping, but did not gainsay the others.

The next morning the maid helped Jane and Fanny into their walking dresses. Jane's was one of her most modish outfits, of soft yellow muslin with contrasting sleeves of orange. She wore matching orange boots and carried a yellow parasol. Fanny's dress was of apricot jaconet with a skirt hem bordered with tucks.

They were quite satisfied with the appearance they made until they went downstairs and saw Lady Juliette. She looked ravishing in a striped blue silk walking dress with a gathered flounce, the darkest of the stripes matching the blue of her eyes. Jane looked at Fanny and gave an almost imperceptible shrug. They could never hope to rival Lady Juliette's beauty and style.

However, Lord Blackwood and Jamie seemed to find nothing wrong with the appearance of the sisters, and complimented them sincerely on their looks. Lord Blackwood was looking wonderful himself, in fawn-coloured pantaloons and blue coat. Jamie was looking top-of-the-trees in pantaloons with a military braid down the side and a tight canary coat.

The group left the house and walked down to the Steyne, where they joined the other fashionables in their daily promenade. It was quite a colourful parade, particularly with all the military uniforms with their bright blues, yellows, reds and plumed helmets and shakos in evidence.

After they had walked a short way, they came to a view of the east facade of the Royal Pavilion, the Prince's preferred home.

"How beautiful!" Fanny exclaimed involuntarily, stopping to admire it, and Jane silently agreed. The Pavilion stretched across an expanse of lawn, looking, with its ornate decoration, like something straight out of a fairy tale. Delicate spires, minarets and onion domes rose into the sky, and below rounded archways were surrounded with filigreed arabesques.

A tinkling laugh interrupted Jane's contemplation of the Pavilion.

"How charming she is," Lady Juliette said, her tone implying the opposite. "Such freshness to be so impressed by the Pavilion."

Lady Martin sniffed, turning to look in the other direction as if the very existence of the building offended her. "It can only be impressive to those from the provinces who have not an educated taste. It is far too overdone."

Fanny flushed and Jane looked at Lady Martin angrily, as did Jamie and Chris. Jane wondered, not for the first time, why Edward seemed not to notice the acid comments of Lady Martin, usually directed at them. At least he seemed not to notice, as he never said anything in their defence.

"The Prince would be flattered by your admiration, Miss Fanny," Lord Grandville said with a smile. "Would you care to see the inside?"

"Oh, yes, how?" Fanny breathed, Lady Martin's unkind comment forgotten. "Do you know the Prince?"

"I am not one of his intimates, but as I have been living here in Brighton the past year, I know him well enough. I had arranged for all of us to tour the Pavilion this morning, but as Lady Juliette and Lady Martin don't care for it, I am sure Lord Blackwood and Mr. Tremaine or Mr. Archer will stay and bear them company."

Adrian, Chris and Jamie agreed to stay with Lady Juliette and her aunt while the other four toured the Pavilion. Jamie and Chris had no real interest in it, being far more fascinated with the fashions exhibited by the gentlemen parading by.

Jane and Fanny took their leave from the others and began to walk up the curving drive to the Pavilion with Lord Grandville and Edward.

"It is not yet finished, you know," Lord Grandville said as they walked through the expanse of lawn and past beds of brightly coloured flowers. "The Prince keeps coming up with new ideas for decorating it, and I rather doubt it will *ever* be done to his complete satisfaction, but I think you will enjoy it."

Lord Grandville spoke to the Prince's secretary inside the Pavilion, and they were allowed to wander through many of the rooms at will. Jane and Fanny thought the interior even more enchanting than the outside. The Prince had given his imagination free rein, and had furnished the rooms in various styles, from the French to the Oriental.

Jane was particularly impressed with a corridor decorated in the Chinese style. The walls were covered in an exquisite hand-painted Chinese wallpaper, the colours of which were also found in the thick Oriental carpet beneath their feet. Large niches in the walls held statues of Chinese gentlemen clad in long robes and displaying sweeping mustaches. Beautifully carved benches upholstered in silk brocade lined the hall, and gaily coloured tasselled lamps hung from the ceiling.

"It's like travelling to China without the trouble and expense," Jane said as she laughed, looking with interest at one of the statues. "I think it is most wonderful."

Edward, who also had not been inside Brighton Pavilion before, agreed. "The Prince has an unmatched imagination and an artist's eye," he declared.

"Yes, and something else, more rare, which is an ability to recognise talent in others," Lord Grandville added as they left the Chinese corridor and passed into a large room with pillars in the shape of palm leaves and marble stairs flanked by wrought-iron balustrades in the shape of bamboo. "The architect John Nash is assisting the Prince in carrying out his ideas for the design and decoration of the Pavilion. Mr. Nash was a relatively unknown architect when Mr. Repton, the landscape artist the Prince had hired to design the Pavilion gardens, had him design a conservatory for the Pavilion. The Prince was very impressed with Mr. Nash's design, and made his interest in the architect known. Now Mr. Nash is not only helping the Prince here at the Pavilion, but is also assisting him with other architectural plans the Prince hopes to carry out."

"I have heard the Prince also encourages artists by giving them his patronage," Fanny commented.

"Not only artists, but also writers and musicians," Lord Grandville corroborated. "So often a talented person is jealous of others with greater talent, but the Prince has no such meanness of spirit."

Jane was sorry when they completed their tour and went to find the rest of their party. The outing was much more enjoyable without the presence of Lady Juliette and her aunt. She hoped they might miss the others and be able to continue as they were, but she was not in luck. They discovered the rest of the party not far from the Pavilion.

Jane wondered if Fanny regretted finding the others as much as she did. During the tour of the Pavilion both Edward and Lord Grandville had been attentive to Jane and Fanny, but now the attention of both shifted subtly to Lady Juliette. Jane was sure Fanny liked the earl, and was puzzled as to why his attentions to Lady Juliette never seemed to bother her. It certainly upset her to see Edward so attentive to Lady Juliette.

Jamie insisted they all go down to the beach to observe the bathing machines closely on their way back to Lord Grandville's town house. They stood together and watched interestedly as the small wooden chambers on wheels were drawn into the sea by patient horses until the floor of the chamber was level with the water. Then the attendant switched the horse to the other end and knocked upon the door of the compartment, which was facing seaward.

"Now the people in the compartment can open the door to the sea and get into the water," Jamie explained to Fanny.

"I should like to try it," Fanny said. "I'm sure the sea water must be beneficial."

"Many think so," said Lord Grandville. "And you could be seen by the Prince." He pointed to a hill where something glinted in the sunlight. "He and his friends often go there with spyglasses to watch the ladies bathing."

Fanny laughed. "I wonder why—the bathing dresses are very concealing."

"Perhaps he looks through the windows of the machines into the compartments," Lord Blackwood said to Jane, *sotto voce*.

Jane felt herself flush at this improper comment and looked askance at Lord Blackwood, who smiled at her devilishly. Lord Blackwood had not attempted to kiss her again since the dinner at the Archers', but Jane felt some of his looks and words were more suggestive than actions. She was not quite sure how she felt about the viscount. She was attracted to him, but he made her feel uncomfortable and somehow apprehensive.

Chris proposed the group lunch at one of the inns near the sea, and Jane seconded the proposal, grateful for the interruption.

After the lunch, they walked slowly back to Lord Grandville's town house, arriving in time for tea. As they waited for the tea, they discussed the day.

"Perhaps tomorrow we shall be able to go shopping if you and your sister have finished gawking," Lady Juliette said to Jane in a low voice.

"I am sorry we kept you from your shopping," Jane replied equably, but Fanny looked at Lady Juliette resentfully.

A maid wheeled in the tea service, and Lady Martin presided over the teapot. As she handed a cup to Fanny, who sat on the far side of Lady Juliette, Fanny seemed to falter and sloshed a little into Lady Juliette's lap.

"You clumsy fool," Lady Juliette said, leaping up and looking down at the stain on her blue silk dress.

"Please forgive me, Lady Juliette," Fanny said, her large eyes filling with tears. "I fear I have overexerted today. I find I am quite shaky. I must not be as robust as I thought yet."

"I cannot think that it is beyond your strength to hold a teacup," Lady Juliette said caustically.

Jane saw the disapproving looks on the faces of the others, except Lady Martin and Lord Blackwood, whose expression was purposely bland.

"I say, Lady Juliette, it was not Fanny's fault. She is not fully recovered from her illness!" Jamie was moved to exclaim.

Lady Juliette, realising the sentiment was in favour of Fanny, modified her tone, but left the room, followed by Lady Martin. Jane looked at Fanny in puzzlement. For a moment she had thought Fanny's action deliberate, but seeing her tear-filled eyes, Jane found it was difficult to believe. Fanny appeared quite crushed by her clumsy action. Perhaps she had not regained as much strength in the past weeks as Jane had thought.

"Why don't you go to your bedchamber and rest awhile before dinner," Jane suggested quietly. She led Fanny from the room, followed by expressions of concern from the others.

THE NEXT MORNING, Lord Grandville and Edward excused themselves from the planned shopping expedition, claiming business they had to attend to. Lord Blackwood, Chris and Jamie professed themselves willing to act as escorts, and they set out with the four women for the shops of Brighton. It was Lord Blackwood who ended up being their escort, for Jamie and Chris disappeared into the tailor's to order some of the new trousers they had seen the day before, determined to be the first in their district of Sussex to wear the most current fashion.

The women and Lord Blackwood went to the haberdashers. Jane and Fanny, used to the limited selection in Staplefield, were much impressed by the availability of fine yard-goods, and even the presence of Lady Juliette and her aunt did not dim their enthusiasm.

There were pastel foulards, rich-looking *gros de Naples*, delicate jaconets, fine valencias and exquisite tulles. Their enthusiasm did dim a little at the prices, but Lady Juliette spent freely, ordering brightly coloured fine silks for her costume. She would not tell what it was to be, but said her maid was going to make it up so that she could be sure it would remain a secret until the night of the masquerade.

Jane and Fanny accepted that they could not purchase much, but they did buy some jonquil-coloured jaconet for new frocks. Fanny also bought a new shawl of fine wool, and Jane allowed herself to be persuaded to buy a length of pale pink sarcenet that Lord Blackwood insisted would flatter her complection.

Lady Juliette seemed in her element among the fashionable shops, and the sisters were surprised to find themselves actually enjoying her company. They went from the haberdasher's to the milliner's and the jeweller's, returning to Lord Grandville's house laden with parcels and with more to be delivered.

EDWARD AND LORD GRANDVILLE set out together, in walking dress consisting of blue coats, buff pantaloons, silk hats and carrying canes. Lord Grandville parted from Edward to go to the Royal Pavilion. As a titled member of the aristocracy, he was expected to pay his respects to the Prince when in Town. Edward went on into Brighton where he had an appointment to meet Sir Howard at a coffeehouse to discuss Sir John Moore.

Edward knew instinctively who Sir Howard was when he saw a distinguished-looking gentleman of about five-and-thirty at a table by a window and went to introduce himself.

"Captain Edward Tremaine, at your service," Edward said with a bow.

"Sir Howard Douglas," the man responded, standing and grasping Edward's hand firmly. He invited him to sit and ordered more coffee.

"I understand from Colonel Fisher that you are concerned with the traducement of Sir John Moore," Sir Howard said.

"Yes, I served under him on the Peninsula, and cannot as an honourable man accept the calumny being heaped unjustly on my former commander."

"It's a sentiment that does you credit, but not one shared by many, I am afraid," Sir Howard said with a sigh. "Have you seen the most recent articles?" he asked, handing Edward a newspaper.

Edward read the article Sir Howard indicated, and a wrathful expression came over his face.

"Bonaparte-struck! They dare to say that Sir John was Bonaparte-struck!" He brought his fist down upon the table in his anger and frustration.

"It's not only what's being written in the papers," Sir Howard informed him. "Why, the only monument that's been put where he fell was erected by the Spanish commander. Country's gone Wellesley-mad and blaming all that's wrong on Sir John. Not that Wellesley isn't a fine general, but if he hadn't inherited the situation he did from Sir John he'd not have been as successful."

Sir Howard shook his head sadly. "It's a sad commentary on us when the only ones to do an English commander justice are foreigners. At least the French give him credit for his accomplishments."

Edward's face looked bleak. "What can we do? I tried talking to Canning and Castlereagh."

"You'll get nowhere with those two. I've given it a great deal of thought, and I believe the Prince is the only way to go. Do you know anyone with his ear?"

"The only person I know with the Prince's ear has no connection with the military," Edward said glumly, thinking of Lord Grandville.

"Well, I have a slight acquaintance with him. If I can't find anyone with more influence I plan to place the case before him myself." He took a sheet of paper and a pen from his pocket. "I'll need as much information as possible. Would you be willing to tell me what you know about the campaign?"

"Gladly," Edward said, happy at last to be able to do something, however little. He told Sir Howard of his experience with Sir John on the Peninsula.

"Do you know what Sir John said just before he died?" Edward finished bitterly. "'I hope my country will do me justice.'"

The two men sat in silence a moment, thinking of Sir John's ironically prophetic words as he lay dying.

"Tremaine. What are you doing in Brighton?" a voice hailed. "I thought you'd be up in London."

Edward looked up in surprise at Colonel Wentworth.

"London?" he asked after introducing Colonel Wentworth to Sir Howard. "Why London?"

"Didn't you get my letter telling you about James Moore and suggesting you make the trip to see him?"

"Sir John's brother?" Sir Howard asked.

"Yes," Colonel Wentworth answered, sitting down at the table. "He's concerned about the defamatory things being said of his brother and plans to write a book to vindicate him. I thought you might be able to help—give him some information he might not get otherwise."

Edward looked puzzled. "I did not receive a letter. I thought you'd been unable to assist me. Very odd."

"Advise you to question your servants, although it's possible it was lost. Well, no great harm done. Here," he said, borrowing Sir Howard's paper and pen, "I'll give you his direction now and you can write."

When Edward left the coffeehouse an hour later, James Moore's direction safe in his coat, he felt more optimistic about clearing Sir John's name than he had in weeks, but he was mystified about the letter. What had happened to it?

THAT AFTERNOON as she sat in the drawing room having tea, Jane was amused to see that Lady Juliette seated herself as far away as possible from Fanny. She wished to avoid any more accidents, Jane supposed.

While they were discussing the day's purchases with Jamie and Chris, who were wearing their new trousers, Lord Grandville returned. He was carrying two small parcels, which he handed to Jane and Fanny, smiling broadly.

"I spoke to the Prince and told him of your admiration of the Pavilion. He was highly gratified and insisted on sending you each a small token."

Curiously, Jane and Fanny opened their parcels. They contained exquisite fans of painted silk and ivory, identical except for their colour. The sticks of the fans were of delicately pierced ivory, and the ivory guards were beautifully inlaid with mother-of-pearl. Even the most particular could not deny they were in excellent taste, and Lady Juliette and her aunt had disgruntled expressions on their faces as the others admired the Prince's gifts.

That evening Lady Juliette, her aunt, Lord Blackwood and Edward went to attend an assembly, but Jane and Fanny begged to be excused. The day's shopping had fatigued them, and they had to rise early the next morning for the journey back to Staplefield.

The next day as the party gathered and waited for the servants to load their luggage, Jane noticed the earl was once again clad in his old-fashioned clothes and wig.

"By the mass, I find I am coming to prefer these styles," he proclaimed. "I'd as leif be comfortable, and loose is more comfortable than the new tight fashions."

"Is it really necessary for you to speak as well as dress three-score years out of fashion?" asked Lady Juliette waspishly, by now suspecting the accent was put on for her benefit.

Jane looked at Lady Juliette in surprise. Lady Juliette was usually most circumspect in her behaviour around the earl.

"Odd words and expressions, Lady Juliette, what do ye mean?" Lord Grandville asked, an innocent expression on his face.

Lady Juliette bit her lip and walked to her carriage, not trusting her temper. She was tired from the late night and unhappy to be returning to the country. Edward and Parkins climbed into the carriage after her.

As they rolled on their way back to Staplefield, Edward stared out the window broodingly. He wished he were recovered enough to ride horseback instead of being forced to ride in a carriage, even if it was with Lady Juliette. Although it had been heartening to find there were others interested in clearing Sir John's name, it was a puzzle about the missing letter. He would have to question Dawkins.

"What are you thinking of so seriously?" Lady Juliette asked, a trace of ill temper still evident in her voice.

Edward turned to her with a smile, recalled to his manners.

"Please forgive my inattention, Lady Juliette. It is just that I am disturbed by something I found out in Brighton." He went on to explain about the letter.

Hoping no trace of guilt showed in her face, Lady Juliette tried to persuade Edward to let the matter drop.

"Why don't you forget the whole thing? If it has turned out well, and it evidently has, what is the difference? Now you have learned the brother is going to vindicate Sir John, you should forget it. Leave it to him."

At first Edward was shocked at her seemingly unfeeling words. Then he realised that a woman could not be expected to understand how an officer would feel about his commander. Although, a voice in the back of his mind said, Jane had.

"It would not bc honourablc for mc to do that, Lady Juliette," he explained gently. "Besides, I may be able to give James Moore information he would otherwise lack."

"Well, if you feel you must," Lady Juliette replied impatiently, sick to death of the subject. She thought that if it weren't for the fact that she wished the earl to think Edward was still competition, she would rather ride with her aunt, whether the Hamptons had a chaperone or not. Edward was extremely poor company.

Her thoughts went to the earl, and his reappearance in his old-style clothes this morning. When she married him she would insist he contest the will and stop wearing those ridiculous fashions. *She* was certainly not going to wear hoops, panniers and wigs.

Edward also wished he were riding with another. He thought again of Jane and how warm and understanding she was. Then he looked guiltily at his travelling companion and forced himself to be more charitable to Lady Juliette. No doubt a great deal of Jane's compassion came from her upbringing as a vicar's daughter. He could not blame Lady Juliette for her different background. But there were certainly aspects of her personality he did not care for. Although, he told himself, there were probably things about any woman he would not like if he got to know her well enough. He sighed inaudibly and settled down for a long, boring journey home.

CHAPTER ELEVEN

ONE OF THE FIRST THINGS Edward did upon returning to Haverton Park was to question Dawkins about the letter. He excused himself from the morning ride and called Dawkins into the library where they would not be overheard.

"Dawkins," he asked, "do you remember a letter about two weeks ago that came from Colonel Wentworth?"

Dawkins, sensing the question was important, thought carefully before answering.

"Yes, Captain Tremaine, I do recall such a letter. It was with several others on the salver in the hall. I was just going to take them up when Lady Tremaine required my presence. When I went back, it was missing. I assumed you had seen it and taken it from the salver. I am sorry if I did wrong," he finished, looking stricken at the idea of having provided anything but the very best of service.

"No, it is of no consequence," Edward assured him. "Perhaps it fell behind a piece of furniture or was taken by accident," suggested Edward.

"I do recall passing Lady Juliette Blackwood in the hall, but no one else."

Edward thanked Dawkins and dismissed him. Lady Juliette, he mused. Could it be possible? But why would she take a letter from Colonel Wentworth? He dismissed the thought as unworthy, deciding it was a mystery that would remain unsolved, but his thoughts remained on Lady Juliette.

He sat in a wing-back chair upholstered in green brocade and leaned back into it thoughtfully. When he had invited Lady Juliette to Haverton Park in July, he had fully intended that her visit end in a proposal of marriage. Now—now he realised he did not wish to make her an offer. The past six weeks had brought out aspects of her character he did not care to see in one to be his wife.

He stared blindly at the book-lined wall. Lady Juliette was beautiful; no one could deny that. She was also a superb horsewoman, a talented musician and a witty conversationalist when she chose to be. But he was beginning to think she lacked what he felt was most important—a heart.

An accumulation of small incidents had disclosed her lack of compassion and kindness. There was her jealousy of other women, her impatience with anyone or anything not directly concerned with herself, and most of all, the way she allowed her aunt to make unkind comments to the Hamptons. There was also the mystery of the letter. He could not be sure, of course, but it was odd. And he was not blind to the way she flirted with the earl. At first he had thought it was just her nature, but he knew now that she would much rather receive an offer from Lord Grandville than from him.

The question was, was he obliged to make an offer after inviting her here? There had been nothing that passed between them that could not bear the closest scrutiny, and they had been well-chaperoned by both her aunt and his mother. But he would not wish to do as Jamie had done to Fanny. Although to tell the truth, he was not sure she would accept an offer if he *did* ask. Not if she thought she might receive one from the earl. The door opened, interrupting his train of thought, and Lady Tremaine entered.

"Dawkins said he thought I would find you here," she said. "I hope I am not disturbing you?"

"No, you are not disturbing me," Edward said, standing. Lady Tremaine sat down gracefully in a comfortable chair and Edward took the one next to her.

"In fact," he said, looking seriously into his mother's hazel eyes, "I have need of your counsel."

He paused a moment, and Lady Tremaine waited patiently for him to speak.

"Do you think I must offer for Lady Juliette, Mother? I believe she suspects I asked her to Haverton with that intention, but I find on closer acquaintance with her that she is not the kind of woman I should like to have as my wife."

An expression he could only interpret as relief crossed his mother's face.

"No, I don't think you must offer. You have conducted yourself with the utmost propriety at all times.

An invitation to an estate for the summer months does not constitute a betrothal,'' she said reassuringly.

''To tell the truth, I am glad you have decided not to offer,'' she continued. ''I have some news I had feared might upset you, and now I suspect it will not. Lady Juliette told me this morning after breakfast that Lord Grandville has invited her to remove to Bramleigh this week when his other guests begin to arrive for the masquerade. She said she plans to accept the invitation since it will give us more room with Mary and her family coming to visit. There's no denying it will, for Haverton Park is not a large house, but I doubt it's her real reason,'' Lady Tremaine finished skeptically.

Edward smiled wryly. So Juliette's interest in the earl was plain for all to see. He wondered at Lord Grandville's extending the invitation. Odd, under the circumstances.

''I rather think Juliette is going to catch cold at that particular game,'' he said. ''I believe I have detected a partiality for Miss Fanny in the earl.''

''I have, as well,'' his mother continued, ''but I suppose Lady Juliette does not fear competition from a simple country miss.''

Lady Tremaine felt a little ashamed for being uncharitable to a guest in her home, and flushed. Edward smiled at her understandingly, and with a laugh Lady Tremaine went back downstairs to Lady Martin.

FEELING AS IF an immeasurably great weight had been lifted from his shoulders, Edward went to his bedchamber to dress in his riding clothes and join the party on their ride, after all. He rang for Ames and his glance fell upon the book lying on the desk beneath the window.

He remembered that first day in June when he had placed the rose from Jane between its leaves. Curious, he opened the book and took out the rose, now brittle, the edges browned, the centre darkened to a deep purple. He held it gently, thinking of Jane. Now there was a woman with a kind heart. He thought of the letter to the Bishop of Salisbury, her help in entertaining his guests despite their unkindness to her and her sharing in his joys. He wished he could find someone like her to be his wife.

The thought repeated itself, and he looked up, astonished that he had been so blind. Jane was the woman for him. That was why he had been so disturbed by Adrian's attentions towards her, and Lady Martin's and Juliette's unkindness. He remembered the times he had ruthlessly suppressed a desire to take her in his arms and kiss her.

He walked back and forth across his chamber and impatiently rang for Ames again. Now that he realised where his affections really lay, he wanted to go to her immediately and place his heart at her feet.

But then as he waited for Ames he realised he couldn't just go to her with such a declaration. It would not be proper while Lady Juliette was still his guest, and how could he even know that Jane would return his feelings? Perhaps she truly cared for Lord Blackwood. A fear clutched his heart as he remembered the kiss he had interrupted in the Archers' garden and the looks he had often noticed Lord Blackwood giving her when he thought he was unobserved. Well, he thought, staving off the fear, he would win her from Lord Blackwood even if her affections did lie there.

The door opened and Ames came in, breathless. "Forgive me, Captain Tremaine, I didn't think you would be needing my services and I was pressing your cravats."

"I don't need you, after all," Edward said, absently toying with the shirt frill at his wrist.

Ames returned to the lower regions of the house wondering what had got into his master. He was not usually so changeable.

THE BLACKWOODS and their aunt departed three days later for Bramleigh. Lord Grandville's other guests had begun to arrive, and his aunt from Devon had come to act as his hostess. Lady Juliette took her leave of Edward quite charmingly, as though all she had ever intended was that they be friends. Edward saw Lady Martin depart with relief, but felt he might actually miss Lord Blackwood's amusing presence.

The next day his sister Mary and her family arrived. The arrival of a family with two young children and their nurse kept the Tremaines from feeling lonely at the departure of the others. For some unaccountable reason, Edward found himself more interested in his sister's children than he had been when he had first seen his nephew. He spent quite a lot of time in the nursery with Tad and Lydia, earning himself several perceptive looks from his sister's green eyes.

He was playing with Tad one morning when Dawkins searched him out in the nursery with the message that he had company below.

"Who?" Edward asked,

"A gentleman," Dawkins replied. "He preferred I not announce his name."

Curious, Edward returned Tad to the care of his nurse and went down to the Green Drawing Room.

"Sir Howard!" Edward exclaimed as he entered the room, striding forward to clasp his hand firmly. "This is a pleasure." Dawkins, anticipating his master's order, came in with a bottle of their best claret and two crystal glasses.

"What brings you to this part of Sussex?" Edward enquired as Sir Howard gratefully drank his claret. "Do you have news on the business of Sir John?"

"As a matter of fact, I have," Sir Howard said with a smile. "I had my audience with the Prince."

Edward leaned forward in his chair. "And?"

"He was most receptive. I summarised the situation to him and he promised to look into the matter of a permanent memorial, at least."

"Do you think he will?"

"Yes. I know he is rather capricious and prone to promise more than he can deliver, but he did seem sincerely concerned about England's failure to do Sir John justice. Of course, there is little we can do about the other. We must look elsewhere to have his name cleared for posterity. Have you been in touch with James Moore?"

Edward refilled Sir Howard's glass. "Yes. He intends to publish some of Sir John's letters this year and begin work on a longer book. He plans to do extensive research for the book and doubts he will finish it for several years. I shall make a trip to see him later and give him what information I have. I suppose we must trust to the book to preserve the truth for posterity."

The two men sat sipping their claret in silence several minutes, thinking of what a fine man Sir John had been and how unjust it was that he should be so little valued for his contributions on the Peninsula.

"At least the Prince's promise is a step forward," Edward said. "I can't thank you enough for bringing me the news personally. You'll stay a few days, surely."

Sir Howard shook his head regretfully. "No, I'm sorry, but I must be on my way today. I have urgent business in London."

"You will at least stay to lunch, will you not?" Edward persisted.

"Yes, thank you," Sir Howard agreed, "I shall be pleased to join you for lunch."

Edward sent Dawkins to ask his father to join them, and the three men became engrossed in a conversation on politics as they waited for lunch to be served.

THE NEXT MORNING Edward decided to begin his campaign to win Jane's affections. The departure of the Blackwoods for Bramleigh had removed any awkwardness he might have felt if Lady Juliette had still been in residence at Haverton Park, and he did not wish to delay too long. Memories of the kiss between

Jane and Lord Blackwood still made him uneasy and he did not want to give Lord Blackwood time to make more progress in gaining Jane's affections.

Edward had thought a great deal about how to approach Jane, and he decided the best way would be to reestablish the custom of the comfortable morning visits they had enjoyed before his trip to London and his meeting Lady Juliette. Once he had restored the close friendship with Jane, he could move to capture her affections and declare himself.

He prepared for this first meeting since his realisation of his feelings for Jane with care, changing his breeches and coat several times, almost driving Ames to distraction. Edward finally decided on buff pantaloons, a white waistcoat, green morning coat of superfine and glossy-top boots. As he viewed himself for perhaps the fortieth time that morning in the mirror, Edward realised sheepishly that he was displaying as much concern about his appearance as Jamie would. Yet he could not help but feel satisfaction that the image presented to him in the glass showed such a great change from that which had confronted him the day he had arrived at Haverton Park from hospital. He gave his cravat a final tug and decided it was time to leave for the Hamptons' or the morning would be past.

Edward arrived at the Hamptons' cottage shortly and was pleased to see Jane in the garden, although she was not at work, but sitting on the bench with her cat in her lap. She seemed to sense his presence, and turned her head towards him, smiling in welcome and moving to rise.

"No, please do not get up, Miss Hampton," Edward begged, as he let himself in the gate. "Thomas would never forgive me," he said as he looked at the contented cat, whose eyes had opened slightly at Jane's movement. "I am surprised not to find you at work among your flowers."

"No, I am taking a break from helping my father," Jane explained as she stroked Thomas, coaxing him to go back to sleep. "As Father nears the completion of his book he demands my assistance more frequently."

"Your garden does not seem to be suffering for lack of attention," Edward commented, looking about, appreciating the riot of midsummer colour it presented.

"No, Fanny has helped me occasionally, and I work in it when I can. How is your family?" she enquired. "I hope your sister and her family are recovered from their journey?"

"Yes. The journey did not seem to tire my sister and her husband much, and the children not at all. I trust your father and Miss Fanny are also well?"

"Father is as usual. Fanny is well, too, although she is not here now. I do not know where she went—perhaps to Bramleigh."

As soon as she said the words, Jane wondered if she had touched a tender spot by mentioning Bramleigh to Captain Tremaine. Fanny had told her of the removal of the Blackwoods to Bramleigh several days ago. Poor Captain Tremaine—Lady Juliette had made it very clear whom she preferred. Jane supposed there was really nothing wrong with the move—Haverton Park *was* small, and there was room for dozens of guests at Bramleigh. But somehow she did not believe this would have influenced Lady Juliette if she had not wished it to.

"What makes you look so serious?" Edward asked teasingly, and Jane turned from her thoughts guiltily.

"Nothing," she said. "Forgive me if I am a little abstracted, it is just that I am worried about Fanny," she temporised, realising as she spoke the words that there was some truth in them. "She has been going somewhere almost every day and always manages to avoid telling anyone *where* she has been."

"I think you need not be concerned about your sister. She is a woman of sense. Be glad that she is going about now, after being confined to the house so long," Edward advised, reaching to pet Thomas as he slept in Jane's lap.

Edward's arm brushed Jane's as he stroked the cat, causing a shiver to go down her spine. To cover her reaction to the accidental contact, she changed the subject.

"Have you heard anything about your attempts on behalf of Sir John?"

"Yes, that is one of the things I wished to tell you. Sir Howard came yesterday and informed me that he had spoken to the Prince. He said the Prince was sympathetic and has promised to see about the matter of a monument, at least."

"I am pleased to hear that, but it is less than you had hoped for, is it not?" Jane questioned shrewdly.

Edward stopped stroking Thomas and ran his fingers through his hair, disturbing the carefully arranged locks. "Yes. I had hoped something could be done about clearing his name to the citizenry, but I suppose that would take the cooperation of the press, and the Prince does not have any influence there," he said, thinking of the unflattering light in which the Prince himself was portrayed in the newspapers. "I fear there is a great struggle ahead of me if I persist in trying to clear Sir John's name. Perhaps the book his brother plans to write will accomplish what I have been unable to achieve."

"I never thought about how the writers for newspapers and the authors of books affect the way we think of a public figure," Jane said thoughtfully. "I suppose it is not the first time a man has been unjustly portrayed. It makes one wonder how true the history we learn is."

They sat in silence a moment, reflecting on human nature, until Edward, hoping for a more cheerful discussion, changed the subject.

"My sister, Mary, wishes to see you and your family soon, and wishes to know if you would dine with us at Haverton Park three nights hence."

"We shall be pleased to do so," Jane accepted, and went on to question Edward about his niece and nephew.

As Edward answered her enquiries, he wondered how he was faring in his attempt to regain Jane's friendship and trust. She was responding to his overtures, but he sensed some reserve—a caution which had not been there before. It was not going to be easy to reinstate himself, he thought ruefully, but he persevered. After he estimated a half-hour had passed, he took his leave, declaring his intention of returning the next morning.

When Edward had left, Jane stayed in the garden, wondering why Captain Tremaine had evidently decided to restore their morning visits in the garden. She supposed it must have been because Lady Juliette had deserted him and he felt lonely. The idea of being a substitute for Lady Juliette disturbed Jane, yet she could not be sorry for any reason that caused him to seek her out. She thought how well he had looked this morning, his shoulders filling out his coat, muscular legs outlined by tight pantaloons, and his blond hair shining healthily in the sunlight. How could any woman have willingly left Captain Tremaine?

THAT AFTERNOON Jane had another caller. Lord Blackwood stopped by, and Mrs. Reid showed him into the parlour where Jane and Fanny sat mending linens, Jane having escaped her father's study for the day.

"I have missed our morning rides together," Lord Blackwood said, as Jane rang for refreshments, "so I have sought out your company here. They ride at Bramleigh, of course, but it was your presence that made the rides enjoyable."

His words included Fanny, yet Jane had the feeling he was speaking directly to her. Flattered, she blushed, and Lord Blackwood smiled his devilish smile.

"I have missed your company also," Jane said honestly, looking into his blue eyes. She reflected idly that while he was wearing clothes very similar to the ones Captain Tremaine had worn that morning, they looked very different. One would never mistake Lord Blackwood for a country gentleman, nor could Captain Tremaine pass for a man of fashion.

"Then we must remedy the situation," Lord Blackwood replied to her admission. "Would you come for a drive with me tomorrow afternoon? Lord Grandville has offered me the use of his curricle since he cannot use it while he is in residence at Bramleigh."

"I should enjoy that." Jane accepted, as Mrs. Reid brought in refreshments.

Lord Blackwood accepted a glass of claret, and they spoke of less personal things, Fanny joining the conversation, as well.

After Lord Blackwood left, Jane wondered just what to think of him. There was no denying she felt an attraction to him, but it was not a comfortable or even a willing attraction. Of her two callers, she much preferred the company of her morning one.

WHEN THE NIGHT of the dinner with the Hamptons arrived, Edward had made two more morning calls on Jane. She appeared to have waited for his visits in her garden, but he still felt a reserve in her which he was at a loss how to overcome. He watched her now at the table speaking to his mother while Fanny visited with his sister, Mary. Mary had known of Fanny's betrothal to Jamie and the subsequent disgraceful actions on his part, and had been anxious to assure herself of Fanny's recovery from the whole affair.

Edward remarked how much more pleasantly the dinner passed without the presence of the Blackwoods and their aunt. Lord Blackwood had been an amusing conversationalist, but things were much nicer without the catty remarks of Lady Martin and Lady Juliette. Squire Deane, his sister's husband, was a hearty companion, and his diverting stories even had the power to keep Mr. Hampton from vanishing into the library. It was a comfortable family dinner, Edward thought, and understood why his father had eschewed the city in favour of his country estate all these years.

After the gentlemen rejoined the ladies in the drawing room, Edward asked Jane to walk in the garden, thinking to continue his campaign to win her affections. Haverton Park's old-fashioned gardens were full of walks, and Jane delighted in the sweet evening smells of the gillyflowers, tuberose and vesper campion.

"Evening is my favourite time in the garden," she said, leaning down to smell the campion more closely.

"I shall always associate you with gardens." Edward smiled, thinking she looked like one of the flowers herself with her pink complection and clad as she was in a pink-sprigged muslin gown with matching ribbands. He bent down, picked a creamy-white tuberose and placed it in Jane's soft brown hair. He saw her breasts rise and fall as his action made her breath quicken, and he had a strong desire to enfold her in his arms and bury his lips in her luxuriant hair. To distract himself, he spoke of Jamie.

"It would seem my brother has permanently lost your sister's affections. However he tries to attract her attention, she persists in ignoring him."

"Yes," Jane said, laughing, thinking of how Jamie had sulked through dinner when Fanny ignored his gallantries. "I believe Fanny has tried several times to get him to agree to end their betrothal, but he refuses."

"I can't say I blame Fanny," Edward said with a smile, "but I'll miss the connection to your family."

They had reached a small fountain and by mutual consent stopped and sat on its edge, sharing the night peace. Edward, knowing he was making a mistake, but unable to stop himself, reached out and took Jane's hand.

"Jane, our families could still be connected if you would marry me."

For one delirious moment Jane was overjoyed, but anger soon followed. She knew why he was asking her for her hand. Because Lady Juliette had refused him, preferring the earl with his higher income and title.

"How dare you ask me to be your wife because Lady Juliette refused you and removed to Bramleigh?" she cried, snatching her hand away from his.

Edward's eyes opened wide in astonishment at this reaction to his proposal. "I did not ask Lady Juliette for her hand," he protested. "I realised it was you whom I loved and wished to marry before Lady Juliette ever left Haverton Park, but I couldn't ask you while she was still here. It would not have been proper."

"Do you expect me to believe that?" Jane said, standing up. She felt the flower he had placed in her hair brush her forehead, and she snatched it out, throwing it angrily into the fountain. "Do you think I have forgotten why you invited her here to Bramleigh? You told me yourself. Do you take me for a fool?"

Edward stood up, as well, and reached for Jane's arm, wishing to calm her.

"Yes, it's true I did invite the Blackwoods here because I thought I loved Juliette, but I came to see tha I did not," he tried to explain. "It is you I love."

"Forgive me if I find that difficult to believe," Jan replied. "You are just like Jamie. It is only your pride. Well, I assure you you will recover just as easily as h will."

She pulled away from him and walked swiftly to th house, her indignation apparent in her stiff posture Edward followed, feeling bewildered by her reaction But as he reflected upon it, he began to understand and cursed himself for speaking too precipitately. H *had* told her why he'd invited Lady Juliette to Haver ton Park, and how could she know of his change o heart? Somehow he would have to convince her of hi sincerity, but how?

Jane tried to disguise the ill temper Edward's insul ing offer had engendered in her but it was a strain, an she was glad when the evening was over and they we able to go home. She had evidently not disguised he feelings well enough, for when they returned hom Fanny followed Jane to her bedchamber.

"What is it, Jane? You have been acting oddly ever since you came in from the garden with Edward," she said with concern.

"I pray no one else noticed," Jane said, sitting on the edge of her bed.

"I doubt it. I only noticed because I am your sister and know you too well. What did Captain Tremaine do to make you so upset?"

"He made me an offer."

"How wonderful!" Fanny exclaimed, going to Jane to embrace her, but Jane got off her bed and moved away.

"Wonderful?" she said, pacing the floor of her bedchamber. "How dare he! I refused him, of course."

"Refused him?" Fanny questioned in confusion. "Then it was all for nothing."

Jane stopped pacing and looked at her sister sharply. "*What* was all for nothing?"

"It makes no matter now," Fanny said, trying to leave the room, but Jane grabbed her by the arm and held her.

"What? Tell me."

"Lord Grandville and I devised a plan," Fanny confessed. "We decided you would make a much better wife for Captain Tremaine than Juliette, and proposed incidents to make her show her true colours."

Jane was shocked. "How could you? You were the one who warned me Edward had only brotherly feelings for me, yet you discussed my feelings for him with Lord Grandville? How could you?" she repeated wrathfully. "I am mortified. You and Lord Grandville have behaved despicably. That's why you never seemed upset when the earl flirted with Lady Juliette. You had planned it all. Lord Grandville is no better than you—worse, since he is a man and older. How could you encourage him to trifle with someone's affections, particularly after your experience with Jamie?"

"Lady Juliette has no heart to trifle with," Fanny defended herself, pulling out of Jane's grasp. "Lord Grandville's behaviour did not go beyond what is acceptable. If Lady Juliette chose to read more into his actions than was there it is her own fault."

Jane could not completely agree with that assessment of the situation. If Lady Juliette had received no encouragement at all, she doubted she would have lost her interest in Captain Tremaine. The possibility that without Fanny's machinations Lady Juliette might still have been with Edward made Jane grateful against her will, but she still felt Fanny's behaviour had been reprehensible.

"It was highly improper of you to have discussed such things with a stranger."

"Lord Grandville is not a stranger," Fanny protested.

"No, not a stranger," Jane accused. "You seem quite well acquainted with his house as well as his person. Have you been going there unaccompanied?"

"I have done nothing improper. We only wanted to help. You and Captain Tremaine are too polite and proper to allow yourselves to see the truth. If not for us you both would have landed with the wrong people."

"You are no judge of that. If Edward chooses Lady Juliette and I choose Lord Blackwood it is no concern of yours or Lord Grandville's," Jane said, at that moment feeling very affectionate towards Lord Blackwood. He, at least, did not seek her company because the one he cared for more didn't care for him, or discuss her intimate feelings with others.

Fanny left the room with an injured expression on her face, and Jane threw herself face down on her bed, sobbing with anger and mortification at the evening's disclosures.

CHAPTER TWELVE

JANE'S ANGER at Edward, Fanny, and Lord Grandville continued several days. There were moments, however, when she wondered whether she should have accepted Edward's offer, insulting though she had felt it was. Would it not be better to be with someone one loved, even though one were second choice, or to be forever without that person? Her feelings wavered back and forth.

Lord Blackwood came most mornings to call, but Jane declared her preparations for the forthcoming ball at Bramleigh were consuming all her attention and politely declined whatever invitations Lord Blackwood extended. She was happy to have an excuse to stay away from Haverton Park and to avoid Lord Grandville. Although an excuse was all it was. She did not have much interest in the ball, and only planned to wear a rose-coloured domino and mask. Fanny, however, insisted that she go in costume, and suggested Diana.

"Diana," Jane sighed. "There will probably be several Dianas. If I must go in costume, at least think of something original."

"Well, then you will be the best Diana. You are not interested in competing for the prize, anyway."

Lord Grandville had decided to offer two prizes, one to the woman and one to the man who wore the most original and daring costumes.

Jane protested a little longer, but finally gave in. What did it matter if there were several Dianas? She could find respite in anonymity. She gave Fanny the pink sarcenet she had purchased in Brighton and left the construction of her costume to Mrs. Reid and Fanny.

Jane thought her sister seemed overly excited about the masquerade, although perhaps it was just her own lack of interest that made Fanny's seem excessive. Fanny was going as Queen Henrietta Maria, to complement Lord Grandville, who was planning to go as Charles I. Jane was concerned that by wearing matching costumes their mutual affection might appear too public to be considered proper but said nothing. The thought of Lord Grandville and Fanny discussing her feelings for Edward and planning their future together made Jane still angry enough to withhold advice.

LADY JULIETTE SAT on one of the delicately painted Adam chairs in the small circular dining room at Bramleigh and looked at the assembled company with a sigh. It had been most discomfitting to find that Lord Crawford was one of Lord Grandville's guests. She was beginning to wish she had never come to Sussex at all.

Captain Tremaine was not rich enough, and Lord Grandville was proving elusive. She had thought the invitation to Bramleigh had indicated progress, but she was treated just like all the other guests.

At least Lord Grandville had stopped talking to her in those ridiculous old expressions since she'd been at Bramleigh. Though she had concealed her feelings well, she had disliked the earl ever since it had become evident that he was doing it solely for her benefit. To tell the truth, she disliked both Lord Grandville and Edward. She didn't like being made a Maygame of by Lord Grandville, and Edward was much too prosy and boring.

She regarded Lord Crawford with interest. His light blue eyes intercepted the look and he smiled knowingly. He had been very game since he had arrived at Bramleigh, but having assessed the situation he had been careful not to draw attention to their mutual interest and had refrained from paying her any special notice. She looked at his large muscular form straining against his buckskins and olive coat and felt a moment's regret. He might not be as wealthy as Edward and Lord Grandville, but how much more a man he was in other ways!

She forced herself to think of Lord Grandville's wealth and looked about the drawing room, noting his many valuable possessions. Once she was married to him she could go her own way. She looked speculatively at Lord Crawford. Yes, even *that* was possible after she provided Lord Grandville with an heir. Her thoughts cheered her and her brilliant smile returned. She would bring Lord Grandville to the sticking point by the end of the masquerade. She could not fail to gain his notice and win the prize for the most daring costume, she thought complacently as she pictured herself in the exotic costume she and her maid were constructing in the privacy of her rooms.

When all of the guests had rested sufficiently after their lunch and began to disperse from the drawing room, Lady Juliette went to her bedchamber to work on her costume. She sent her maid to find some embroidery silks and tried on the satin cap she was fashioning. She stood before the gilt-framed oval glass and held several ostrich feathers on her cap at different angles in an effort to determine where they looked best.

"Very charming, my dear. Although I think you should add some paste jewels—around the edge and a cluster in the centre, I think."

Lady Juliette gasped and whirled about to face Lord Crawford.

"How dare you enter my bedchamber!" she exclaimed angrily. "If you were seen by anyone you could undo all."

"I assure you no one saw me enter," Lord Crawford said, advancing farther into the room and closing the door behind him. "The gentlemen are gone to the stable to inspect Lord Grandville's cattle, and the ladies are entertaining themselves in the music room."

Lady Juliette did not look reassured by his words, and he endeavoured to set her fears at rest.

"Do not worry, I have no desire to spoil your plans. In fact, I came to assist you in them by giving you a warning. You really must guard the way you look at me in company, my dear, or someone will notice and remember the old rumours."

Lady Juliette flushed at the emphasis he put on the last word and anger at having her thoughts so easily read by him overcame her.

"You flatter yourself, Lord Crawford," she said coldly, turning away.

"I think not," he contradicted and, coming closer, grasped her chin in his hand and turned her face back to his. He gazed steadily into her eyes, and Lady Juliette's expression slowly changed from one of anger to one that was almost flirtatious. Her long black eyelashes swept invitingly down over her cheeks, and her red lips pouted provocatively. Lord Crawford placed his lips over hers in a kiss that quickly became demanding. When he sensed he had aroused a hunger in Lady Juliette, he put her away from him.

"Ah, what memories the touch of your lips awakens," he said, meaningfully. "Are you quite sure you wish to have Lord Grandville? He seems rather a cold fish to me."

His lightly mocking words returned Lady Juliette to an awareness of the danger she was in while Lord Crawford remained in her bedchamber.

"I am sure. Lord Grandville has the wealth to support me in the manner which I desire. You do not. Please leave my bedchamber at once before you are observed."

"If you change your mind, my dear, you have only to let me know," Lord Crawford said as he placed his hand upon the doorknob. "I still think it a pity you have chosen as you have. Or rather a waste. Only a true onnoisseur of women deserves to possess you." With mocking bow and smile, he left the room.

Lady Juliette hastened to close the door behind him nd sank into a chair, still clutching the feathers in her ight hand. She laid them down on a table, thinking hat life was most unfair. Why did a prosy bore such as Edward and a buffoon such as Lord Grandville have wealth, while she and her brother and Lord Crawford ad none? It was decidedly unjust!

WHEN THE NIGHT of the masquerade arrived, Mrs. Reid stayed late to help the sisters dress. Fanny looked nagnificent as Queen Henrietta Maria. Her white satin kirts hung straight and full to the ground from a lightly raised waistline. The three-quarter-length leeves were slashed to expose blue satin beneath and ed below her elbows with blue ribands. Blue rosettes dorned her waist and her dainty white satin slippers. ane looked at her sister in admiration and wished she ad shown more interest in her own costume.

Jane felt embarrassed and almost naked in the costume Fanny and Mrs. Reid had designed for her. The hell-pink sarcenet draperies fell to just above her ankles, clinging tightly to her figure and showing the andals that laced about her limbs with pink ribands. Her hair was curled tightly and rolled up on her head, nd she wore a satin covered quiver of arrows on her ack. As she adjusted the pink silk mask over her face, ane wished it truly disguised her identity.

However, Mr. Hampton, in a black domino and half nask, did not seem to find anything amiss with either of his daughters' costumes. Jane reluctantly decide that if a clergyman did not find her costume indecen she should not, and resigned herself to appearing in i

At Bramleigh, Lord Blackwood knocked upon tl door to his sister's dressing room. Parkins admitte him, and he joined Lady Juliette, who was lookir critically at herself in a gilt-framed mirror.

"Dear sister," Adrian said, looking at his sister beauty appreciatively, "you will be the most beautif woman at the masquerade. Without a doubt you w win the prize. However," he continued, going to lea negligently against the large mahogany wardrobe, " won't avail you anything."

"Tell me what you want and leave so I can finis dressing," Lady Juliette said impatiently, tying tl fringed sash of her Turkish costume at a little diffe ent angle and standing back to judge the effect.

"I wished to inform you that I shall be leaving f the Continent to join Father a few days hence. The is no purpose in remaining here. It will not be yo home. You have lost the game. You let Tremaine g and can't see you are being played for a fool by Lo Grandville."

Lady Juliette looked at him scornfully. "Much yo know about it."

"Perhaps I know more about it than you think Lord Blackwood said warningly. "I have eyes for ot ers besides myself, and I use them. I advise you to c your losses and take Lord Crawford. You have a ready enjoyed his favours, and he seems to be inte ested still. Perhaps that is why Lord Grandville invited him to Bramleigh for the masquerade. He is a most considerate host," he finished with a wicked smile.

Lady Juliette looked at him in fury and threw a silver-backed hairbrush, but he dodged it easily and the mark it left was upon the wardrobe. With a last grin at his sister he went to go don his own costume. His sister *was* a beauty. Too bad she hadn't the understanding of people to use that beauty to real advantage.

THE MASQUERADE was set to begin rather late by country hours—at eight—but as the Hamptons drove up the circular drive to Bramleigh, Jane understood why the earl had chosen that hour. The shrubs and trees about the house had been filled with lanterns in the shape of stars, and in the fading light of the day, Bramleigh was taking on the aspect of a fairyland. As their carriage stopped before the brightly lit residencc, footmen in lively coloured liveries carrying flambeaux came forward to assist them from the carriage. Jane felt a thrill of anticipation despite herself.

Lord Grandville and his aunt stood in the doorway of the ballroom to welcome the guests. His aunt was dressed rather plainly as Rubens's wife, but Lord Grandville, as Charles I, looked quite splendid. He was clad in a blue satin doublet and breeches that tied at the knee with bows. The long full sleeves of his white shirt were slashed from the shoulder to the wrist, revealing pink satin beneath. A large lace-edged collar was turned down over the shirt, and the long dark locks of his wig fell over past his shoulders. Silk hose, square-toed leather shoes decorated with rosettes of pink riband and a wide-brimmed plumed hat completed his outfit. Jane had to admit that he presented a very dashing and romantic figure in the costume of the seventeenth-century king. He welcomed the Hamptons warmly, with a special smile for Fanny, and the family passed into the ballroom to join the rest of the company.

The ground-floor rooms of Bramleigh had all been opened so the guests could wander at will from the ballroom to the withdrawing room, supper room and card room. The rooms had been lavishly decorated with plants, and hundreds of lamps of coloured glass had been placed about, throwing the stucco decorations on the walls and ceiling into relief and casting muted shadows on the guests.

Mr. Hampton, as usual, vanished within minutes of their entering the ballroom. Jane and Fanny had no doubt he could already be found in the library upstairs. They searched resignedly for the Archers, spying them as a Greek noble and his wife with Chris and Marianne as their slaves.

They sat in the gilt chairs by the wall and amused themselves trying to identify the costumed guests. Although they were all masked, they felt they recognised many of their friends. The lady with the russet hair dressed as Queen Elizabeth could only be Lady Tremaine, and the Henry VIII beside her must be Lord Tremaine. Marianne was the first to see Lady Juliette.

"Isn't she beautiful!" she exclaimed, and the others turned to look.

Lady Juliette's costume was very daring indeed, particularly for the country. She wore full pink drawers gathered at the waist with a fringed yellow sash, a low-cut blouse of fine white lawn covered by a blue stole whose ends were caught up at the waist under a jewelled girdle. She completed her costume with a blue feathered cap, embroidered slippers, and a jewelled mask. She looked quite exotic and beautiful, Jane thought somewhat enviously.

Lord Blackwood had entered with his sister, and he was also clad in Turkish dress. He wore baggy trousers of yellow sashed at the waist, a fine cambric shirt and a loose fur-trimmed robe of blue. The brother and sister were attracting a great many looks, both admiring and disapproving. Lady Juliette, if not her brother, was sure to win the prize, Jane thought.

They lost sight of the Blackwoods in the crowd and turned their attention back to the other guests. Jane thought she recognised Edward's sister, Mary, as a shepherdess, and Lady Archer spied Squire Shirley in the costume of a chimney sweep. Jane looked for Edward, but could not spot him, although Fanny saw Jamie, dressed in the colourful costume of a running footman. He wore a bright blue tunic weighted down by a heavy gold fringe, stockings but no breeches, a cap with feathers, and he carried the long cane surmounted with a silver ball that was the running footman's hallmark. Jane wondered if the ball contained the mixture of white wine and eggs that a real running footman's would have. It was even a more daring costume than Lady Juliette's, and Jane hoped he would capture the men's prize.

They amused themselves for quite a long time admiring the costumes. As Jane had predicted, there were several Dianas, although none like hers. There was also a highwayman, Arcadian princess, old woman, Jane Shore and a minstrel, whom none of them had identified by the time the dancing started.

The dancing began with a slow stately allemande Jane was led out by Lord Blackwood, whose eye showed admiration through his yellow silk mask. A she curtseyed to Lord Blackwood, she finally spie Edward, dressed as Richard Coeur de Lion, standin up with Lady Juliette.

So he did not care for Lady Juliette, Jane though angrily. Then why was he standing up with her for th first dance? Anger and jealousy at the sight provoke her to smile enchantingly at Lord Blackwood. Al though she knew Lord Blackwood was aware who sh was, the etiquette of the masquerade prevented eithe openly acknowledging the identity of the other. Thu relieved of any inhibitions, she flirted with Lor Blackwood more daringly than she ever had befor When he led her back to her place by Lady Archer, pressure on her hand and the look in his eyes told he he was going to hold her to the promise of her flirt tious conduct.

The second dance at the Bramleigh masquerade w traditionally a minuet, the most popular dance of th eighteenth century. The former Lord Grandville ha placed it at the beginning of the program so people would watch it before going to play cards or to other amusements. The minuet had gone out of style, for it was an extremely complicated and difficult dance. None of the younger people could master it, and they stood about to watch and admire the older couples as they performed the intricate steps.

The musicians, who were dressed as Arcadian shepherds, were poised to begin the minuet when Lord Grandville went to stand before them and held up his hand for silence. When the rumble of conversation ceased, he held up two objects.

"I should like to announce the winners of the prizes for the most original and daring costumes. I thank you all for entering into the contest with a spirit I know my great-uncle would have admired, for it is reminiscent of that golden age which he so relished."

There was applause, and Lord Grandville bowed, sweeping his plumed hat off gracefully. "Now for the ladies," he said, and unfurled a beautiful fan. From their position near the musicians, Jane could see it was of a silk so fine as to be transparent, and the ivory guards appeared to be ornamented in gold.

"Although every lady here tonight is beautiful, there is no question but that the most original and daring costume is that of the Turkish princess," he proclaimed.

Lady Juliette went forward to claim her prize amidst great applause. As she took the fan from Lord Grandville he bestowed a kiss upon her hand and she curtsied with exquisite grace, obviously in her element.

"For the gentleman," Lord Blackwood continued, "there is an ebony snuffbox." As he held it up, the jewel-encrusted lid glinted in the candlelight. "Again, I believe there can be little argument that the most original and daring costume is that of the running footman."

As Jamie went forward to claim his prize there was more applause, and the crowd waited expectantly for Lord Grandville to motion the musicians to resume playing. Instead, he held up his hand again for silence.

"I have one more announcement I wish to make before the dancing is resumed," he declared. He held out his hand and was joined by Fanny.

"I am pleased to take the occasion of the Bramleigh masquerade to announce my betrothal to Miss Fanny Hampton," he announced.

Jane felt her shock echoed in the other guests around her. Fanny's engagement to Jamie had never been officially declared over, although it had probably been evident to all that it was. The guests were silent for a long moment, and then began to applaud.

Jane stood stock-still, feeling a deep hurt that Fanny had not confided in her, and wondered if their father had been aware of the betrothal. Of course he must have been, she realised. Even Lord Grandville could not be that lost to propriety. Jane concluded the announcement tonight was Fanny's way of calling off the betrothal with Jamie since he wouldn't cooperate, and knew that if Fanny had confided in her she would have tried to dissuade her from the plan.

Lord Grandville signalled the musicians to begin, and he and Fanny led off the minuet. Jane knew then what Fanny had been doing at Lord Grandville's. Learning the minuet was extremely difficult, and they must have practiced many days to have so perfected the dance. Numb, Jane watched as Fanny performed the glides, toe points, bows and dainty steps with exquisite perfection.

Marianne nudged her and nodded in the direction of Lady Juliette, who was standing not far away. She stood viewing Lord Grandville and Fanny with a look of barely concealed fury on her face. Jane felt compassion for her for a moment, but it vanished when Edward went to Lady Juliette's side and remained there, talking to her.

After the minuet, some of the guests left the ballroom to go to the card room, and others wandered through the open doors to the beautifully lit grounds. Fanny rejoined the Archers in company with the earl, looking at Jane a little hesitantly. However, she had nothing to fear, for Jane had abandoned her pique and she and Lady Archer embraced Fanny warmly. Lord Grandville apologised for not confiding in Jane but assured her that Mr. Hampton had been aware of their plans to announce their betrothal tonight.

A cotillion began, and Jane was swept off by the minstrel, whom Jane finally identified as Mr. Fairchild. After that, she was claimed by the chimney sweep, a shepherd and Paris in succession, before being taken to supper by Lord Blackwood.

The earl had not stinted on the refreshments, and after a rich meal of sautéed segments of pheasant with truffles, larks in patty cases, ham in Madeira sauce and lemon sponge, Jane did not feel like dancing again immediately.

By mutual consent, she and Lord Blackwood strolled slowly out onto the grounds. The glowing lights gave a feeling of enchantment to the night, and before long they had wandered quite a way into a grove of trees away from the lights. Jane stumbled over a fallen branch, and Lord Blackwood reached out to steady her, his hands warm on her flesh through the thin draperies of her costume. His hands tightened, and instead of releasing her, he turned her in his arms and kissed her softly on the lips.

The events of the evening had made Jane receptive to romance, and she returned the kiss, thinking, *This is a man who finds me attractive for myself, not because another had refused him*. Her lips parted beneath his, and the viscount became more demanding. Soon, without quite knowing how, Jane found her quiver had been removed and she was lying on the grass beneath Lord Blackwood, being thoroughly kissed. His body was warm and hard against hers, and through a strange misty, languorous sensation, Jane began to feel a little frightened.

"Jane," Lord Blackwood breathed, "I can't do without you any longer."

Jane felt the flimsy draperies of her skirt being pushed aside, and now felt real fear. She attempted to push Lord Blackwood away, but could not fight his superior strength. He held her easily to the ground, his form hard and pulsing against hers. She would have called out, but he kept her silent with a demanding kiss that made it difficult for her to breathe.

The misty feeling was completely gone now, and Jane felt very clear-headed as she fully realised the danger she was in. She had been playing with fire to flirt as she had with Lord Blackwood. She was trying desperately to think how to get away when suddenly his weight was pulled off her and Lord Blackwood lay on the ground a few feet away. Edward stood above him, his face suffused with fury.

"Name your seconds," he demanded.

Lord Blackwood stood up slowly. "There is no need for such barbarism," he said calmly. "This may be settled honourably in another way. Please leave us. I assure you that you may safely do so."

Edward made no move to leave, but went to Jane and helped her up.

"Do you wish to intrude upon a proposal of marriage?" Lord Blackwood added.

Edward still hesitated, and Jane, aware that her uninhibited flirting had contributed to Lord Blackwood's behaviour this evening, seconded Lord Blackwood's request.

"Please, Captain Tremaine. I shall be quite safe now with Lord Blackwood," she said somewhat shakily, brushing off her skirts and trying to return the draperies to their original folds.

Edward looked at her closely, an unfathomable expression in his eyes.

"I shall be within distance of your call," he said, before leaving with a meaningful glance at Lord Blackwood.

When he had gone, Lord Blackwood stepped forward and took Jane's hand, holding it between both of his.

"Please forgive my unconscionable behaviour this night, Miss Hampton. I can only say in my defence that I was truly overcome by your beauty. I offer you my hand in marriage. Please do not feel I only offer because of my reprehensible actions. I truly hold you in great affection and would have offered before if I had felt I could give you the life you deserve. I have no money and a great many bad habits and can only offer you my love. Please marry me and we shall go to the Continent together."

Jane said nothing for a moment after his long speech, trying to think what to do. Should she accept this man? He was charming, handsome, and although he had frightened her tonight, until now he had exhibited nothing but kindness towards her, whatever his past may have been. But if she were to accept Lord Blackwood, she would be condemning him to the very thing she would not accept from Edward—a marriage in which he would be second best.

"I am deeply honoured, Lord Blackwood," she said, making her decision, "but I must refuse your offer."

Lord Blackwood did not seem surprised.

"You love Captain Tremaine, do you not?"

Jane blushed to find her emotions were so easily read by everyone. "Yes," she admitted.

"Forgive me for asking, but why do you not marry him? It is obvious he cares for you," he said rubbing his jaw ruefully where it had recently been in contact with Edward's fist. "I would wager he has offered."

"I won't be second best after your sister," Jane answered honestly. "That's why I won't accept *you*. You also deserve better than second best."

"I would have you, regardless, even knowing that," Adrian said gently. "You are a rare combination of goodness and quality. A man would be honoured to have you as a wife under any circumstances."

Jane knew she was being given a sincere and rare compliment, and it hurt her to cause him such pain. For a moment she was tempted to accept him, but did not give way to the impulse.

"Thank you, Lord Blackwood," she said. "You will always hold a special place in my affections, but I cannot accept your gracious offer."

"Would you like me to order a groom to get a carriage for you?" he asked, honouring her decision as well as honouring her desire to escape scandal owing to the deshabille of her costume.

"Thank you," Jane said gratefully. "And would you please inform my sister and father that I have been overcome by the headache and returned home early?"

"Of course," Lord Blackwood said. "Wait here a few minutes until I can inform the groom, and then go around to the front of the house where the carriage will be waiting."

He stood close to her in the dim light, and took his leave of her with an unexpected kiss on her cheek.

EDWARD STOOD BY A TREE near the path leading back to the house, watching and listening in the direction where he'd left Jane with Lord Blackwood. Following the two faint figures into the grove this evening had been a fortunate impulse. He had sensed somehow that the couple was Jane and Lord Blackwood, and he had not trusted the rakish viscount.

He heard someone coming down the path and saw Lord Blackwood striding towards him without Jane.

"Where's Jane?" Edward demanded, accosting Lord Blackwood.

"Safe," Lord Blackwood replied, attempting to pass Edward.

"Did she accept your offer?" Edward asked, putting his hand on Lord Blackwood's arm to detain him.

"That is none of your affair unless she chooses to make it so," Lord Blackwood replied, removing Edward's hand from his arm. "Now if you will excuse me, I have a message to deliver to her father."

Reluctantly Edward stepped back and Lord Blackwood went on his way to the house. Edward, wanting to assure himself of Jane's welfare, went to search for her. He found her leaning against a tree in the same place he had left her minutes ago. She looked up at him, but said nothing.

"Did you accept Adrian?" Edward asked, his voice rough with anxiety.

"It is no concern of yours," she replied, unconsciously echoing Lord Blackwood's reply, and inflaming Edward's temper.

"I would say it is a concern of mine since I saved you from his importunate embraces not fifteen minutes past," Edward said angrily. "But perhaps you did not wish to be rescued. Perhaps those are the kind of embraces you prefer. If so, I can accommodate you as well as Adrian Blackwood," he finished, dropping down beside her and bearing her down as he gave her a punishing kiss.

Jane again found herself on the ground being kissed demandingly. This time her response was not fear but something new. She desired him to be closer, much closer. Her arms crept about his back, and she pressed against him.

"Jane," he said, lifting his lips from hers, "you do care for me. Marry me, not Adrian."

His words brought Jane to her senses. "No," she said, pushing him away.

For a moment Jane was tempted, but then she remembered Edward dancing with Lady Juliette earlier. Not wanting to be humiliated by being forced to admit she loved someone who did not love her, she remained mute.

Her silence seemed to anger him, and he stood up, pulling Jane with him. His face had lost its passion, and in the dim light she could see he was very angry.

"I am not going to grovel to you and apologise for the rest of my life that I did not realise I loved you earlier, Jane Hampton. Yes, I thought I loved Lady Juliette. She is a very beautiful and charming woman. It took me time to realise that there are other things that are more valuable. But I never asked her to marry me.

If your pride makes you refuse to accept me, you may take it to your bed."

Angrily he released her and went back towards the house, leaving her alone. Jane, shaken, wondered what she had done. She walked slowly in the direction of the front of Bramleigh where the carriage waited for her. The footman's face was inscrutable as he handed her into the carriage, but as he closed the door, Jane noted the curious glint in his eye. She felt a little curious herself. It had been a most confusing night for a lady who had been most reluctant to attend.

CHAPTER THIRTEEN

THE AUGUST SUN rose hot and bright, and Jane opened the windows of her bedchamber as wide as possible, but she was reluctant to go below and face the day. After she had returned home from the masquerade the night before, she had gone directly to her room and sobbed quietly beneath the covers, feeling lonely and unwanted, except perhaps by Lord Blackwood. Thomas had jumped upon the bed and meowed inquisitively, wondering what ailed his mistress. A long time later, she had fallen asleep, holding the cat close, deriving comfort from his warm and undemanding presence.

A light tap sounded at her door, and reluctantly Jane bade her sister enter.

"What is wrong, Jane?" Fanny asked, going to tand beside her. "Why haven't you come down for breakfast yet? I hope you are not angry with me for not elling you of my betrothal to Lord Grandville before it was announced last night. I was afraid you would have tried to dissuade me if I told you of my plans," he confessed.

Jane embraced her sister lightly. "No, I am not anry about that, although I was a little hurt. I probably *would* have tried to discourage you, had I known," she admitted. "Now I realise you felt the only way to end the situation with Jamie was to present him with a *fai accompli*, and perhaps it was."

"Then what is disturbing you?" Fanny persisted. "I know something is, so don't try to fob me off with excuses."

"Nothing," Jane insisted. "It is just that a trace o my headache from last night is lingering."

Fanny looked at Jane skeptically, but did not prob further. "Come downstairs and let me talk to you whil you have something to eat," she said by way of persuasion. "I want to tell you how my betrothal t Charles came about."

As Jane looked at Fanny's happy face, she could no be so churlish as to ruin her sister's joy with her ba temper. She accompanied her to the dining room an ate some bread and rashers while Fanny confided to he that she had been secretly betrothed to Lord Grand ville for six weeks. Jane listened with half an ear, tryin to be glad for her sister, but Fanny's very happines contrasted so sharply with her own misery that it wa difficult to bear.

Early in the afternoon, Lord Blackwood callec Fanny, after a glance at their faces, quite imprope left the two in sole possession of the drawing room.

"Your sister is a perceptive woman, Miss Ham ton," Lord Blackwood said. "I did wish to speak t you privately."

Jane felt a flash of uneasiness, and then wa ashamed of herself. Lord Blackwood was not likely t make unwelcome advances to her in her own drawing room with her father within calling distance. She looked at Lord Blackwood's handsome figure in his claret-coloured coat, frilled white shirt, buff waistcoat, form-fitting pantaloons and shining Hessians.

He smiled a knowing smile at Jane, and again she had the feeling he always knew just what passed in her thoughts.

"I only wished to tell you I am leaving for the Continent on the morrow, and to ask if you would reconsider your decision not to accompany me."

Jane moved as if to speak, and Lord Blackwood held up his hand.

"Please allow me to finish. I know that I would be your second choice, but I accept that. I love you, regardless. I could not promise to be a perfect husband, but I would always cherish you."

"I wish I could accept your offer, but I can't," Jane said a little sorrowfully. "You are leaving tomorrow, hen? I shall miss you," she said sincerely.

Lord Blackwood wished she would miss him enough hat it would persuade her to go with him, but he said no more about it, knowing her decision was final.

"Yes, my sister has already departed, and I see no point in staying myself, kind as Lord Grandville is."

"Lady Juliette has left?" Jane asked in surprise. She would have thought Lady Juliette would stay and try to win Edward back now that Lord Grandville was beyond reach.

"Yes, she and Lord Crawford are on their way to Gretna, if I am any judge."

"Gretna?" Jane repeated, feeling like a parrot repeating Lord Blackwood's every word, but the news was so surprising.

"Actually, I think my sister will be happy with him. He is a rogue, but so is my sister at heart. I know that sounds unkind, but it's true."

Jane experienced a great fondness and admiration for Lord Blackwood. Above all else, he was honest and kind, despite his sometimes deserved reputation.

Lord Blackwood stood. "Well, if I can't convince you to go with me, there is no point in delaying. I'll be on my way."

Jane stood also and Lord Blackwood came forward and took her hands in his.

"Goodbye, Jane," he said, bending to place a last kiss upon her lips.

"Jane," he said, without letting go of her hands, "I shall probably regret this impulse later, but I feel at this moment that I love you so much I wish you to be happy, even at my own expense. Please do not condemn Tremaine for thinking he loved my sister. My sister is the kind of woman few men can resist. Credit him with seeing through her as soon as he did. And I also happen to know that he did *not* offer for Juliette. I doubt he would have, even if my sister had not gone for bigger game in the earl. Don't let your pride keep you from him. Go to him. Pride is a cold bedfellow."

At these last words, so like Edward's of the night before, Jane started.

Lord Blackwood squeezed her hands lightly and left. Jane sat back down and stayed alone in the drawing room a long time, thinking over what Lord Blackwood had said. Perhaps he was right, but she just *couldn't* go to Edward.

FROM HER PLACE by the dining room window, Fanny thoughtfully observed Lord Blackwood leave. She sensed that Lord Blackwood had offered and been refused. There was just one reason for Jane to refuse Lord Blackwood—she still loved Edward Tremaine. She thought back to the night before. Even in the excitement of what had been her betrothal ball she had not failed to notice Jane's early departure. She had also observed the black expression on Captain Tremaine's face when he returned to the ballroom after being gone almost an hour.

It was clear Jane and Edward loved each other and just as clear that they would need help if they were ever to make a match. She pulled a chair from the dining table and sat down to think. It was a situation that called for drastic measures. She would not be able to handle it alone, but she knew who would help her. Charles had not failed her yet.

EDWARD SAT in the cozy Rose Drawing Room with his sister and mother early in the afternoon several days after the masquerade. Viscount Tremaine and Mary's husband had gone to look at some horses Squire Shirley was considering parting with, and Jamie was riding with Chris.

He was thinking about the odd parcel that had arrived from Bramleigh that morning. Not odd, precisely, for it contained the missing letter from Colone Wentworth, and the direction had been written in hand very like Lady Juliette's. So she had a conscienc after all—she must have left it with a servant to be de livered after she was gone. He wondered why she ha taken it to begin with. To keep him in Sussex, per haps? That must have been it—she hadn't wanted hi to leave so that she could continue to have access to th earl. Her plotting hadn't done her much good, h thought, since she had lost the earl to Fanny, anywa He wished Lady Juliette well with Lord Crawford.

"What is on your mind?" Mary asked with son asperity. "That is the third time I have repeated m question."

"I'm sorry, Mary. What did you ask?"

"I asked if you agreed it was a good idea for Jam to accompany George and myself back to Yorkshi until the term begins."

Jamie had been in very bad spirits since the a nouncement of Fanny's betrothal to Lord Grandvi at the masquerade.

"Yes, either that or purchase him a pair of co ours," Edward said. "I'm not sure the university is t place for him. He needs to grow up."

"Let him make that decision," said Lady T maine. "We'll give him a choice when he goes up Yorkshire. He can think about it there."

Dawkins entered the room, interrupting their co versation.

"Miss Fanny Hampton has asked to speak to yc Captain Tremaine," he said. "She says it is most

;ent, and appears to be quite agitated. I have put her n the Green Drawing Room."

Edward looked up in surprise. "I wonder what it :ould be?" he said, and excused himself to find out.

When he reached the door of the Green Drawing Room, Fanny was pacing up and down the length of he room. When she heard his step, she turned and ran ıp to him, her large eyes looking tearfully distressed.

"Oh, Captain Tremaine, you must help me! I think ane has been abducted!"

"Abducted?" A cold fear went through Edward. 'Explain yourself," he commanded rather brusquely.

"Either that or she has run off with Lord Black-/ood, and if so she can't have thought what she is oing," Fanny cried. "I had gone to Staplefield to get ome embroidery silks, and on the way back I saw a losed carriage with its shades drawn go by. It looked dd, but I didn't give it any more thought until I got ome and found Jane gone." She stopped to take a andkerchief from her pocket and wipe her eyes.

"Gone? Is it possible she just went for a walk or on n errand?"

"No," Fanny said. "I checked her wardrobe, and veral items are missing. I didn't know where to turn, I came to you," she cried, hoping that in his agita-on Edward would not stop to wonder why she hadn't ppealed to his father, Lord Grandville or her own ther.

"How long ago was it you saw the carriage?" he ked.

"Two hours."

Two hours. If he left immediately he might be ab to catch them by nightfall. He rang the bell and o dered his father's fastest horse to be saddled an brought round. Thank goodness he had fully r covered his strength.

"What road did the carriage take?" he asked as h waited for the horse.

"The road to Brighton, I think."

"Don't worry, Fanny," Edward reassured her as h watched out the window for his horse, "I'll bring yo sister back safely whether she went of her own free w or has been forcibly taken."

He saw the groom bringing round the horse and ra down to meet him.

Fanny's eyes dried miraculously as she watch Edward mount his horse and take the drive at a fa pace. Then she went calmly upstairs to join his sist and Lady Tremaine.

JANE WALKED SLOWLY along the road to the Archer feeling more irritated with her sister by the minute. S didn't know why Fanny couldn't have gone herself collect the pattern books from Lady Archer, or why s had to have them today. Her wedding to Lord Gran ville would not be for several weeks yet. One or t days' difference would make no matter, and it wa long, hot walk.

She heard a carriage coming up behind and mov to the side of the road. She was surprised when stopped a little way up. Thinking they might want ask directions, she advanced to the coach, but fell ba when the door opened and a man dressed in a long black cloak, mask and wide-brimmed black hat jumped out. Before she knew what he intended, he had grabbed her and thrust her into the carriage, slamming the door and shouting at the coachman to go.

"What is the meaning of this?" Jane demanded, outraged. As she picked herself up from the green velvet squabs where she had fallen, she looked indignantly at her abductor.

"Odds salts and vinaigrettes, my dear, that is not the proper reaction. You are supposed to scream and have a fit of the vapours."

"Lord Grandville, let me down immediately!" Jane fumed. "If this is another prank of yours and Fanny's, I want none of it."

"I'm afraid I can't oblige you, fair damsel in distress," Lord Grandville, for it was he, said cheerfully. "Don't fret, the journey will not be long."

"I should hope not. My father will begin to worry if I'm not home by nightfall," Jane said, making herself more comfortable on the soft cushions.

"That's right," the earl said with approval. "You might as well relax and enjoy the trip." He lifted a basket from the floor and opened it. "Bread and cheese, my dear? Or perhaps a meat pasty?"

Jane ignored the offer of food. "Where are you taking me?"

"That I cannot tell," he replied, removing his mask and eating a meat pasty with apparent relish.

Jane resigned herself to participating in the escapade and took some bread and cheese, but after two hours passed she began to worry.

"You must take me back, Lord Grandville," she insisted. "I haven't the clothes or anything else I need for a journey."

Lord Grandville seemed to be listening intently. "No need, damsel in distress. I believe your rescue is at hand."

Now Jane also heard the sound of more hooves upon the road. Lord Grandville knocked on the roof of the carriage and shouted for the coachman to stop.

"Forgive me if I leave you, but odds bullets and barrels, I've no wish to be shot, and your rescuer may be rather incensed with me."

He threw his hat and cloak on the seat of the carriage and jumped out. Taking the horse the postilion had been riding, he disappeared down the road.

Jane heard a shout, and a horse came round the curve behind them. The horseman stopped and, swiftly dismounting, ran to the carriage door and threw it open.

"So Lord Blackwood got away," he said, looking in the carriage. "He'll not get far before I overtake him. Are you all right?" he added, assisting Jane from the carriage.

"Don't waste your time going after Lord Blackwood," she said dryly, "it was not he." She stretched her legs and walked down the road a little to alleviate the cramps.

"Then who?" asked Edward, but before she could answer, they were distracted by the sight of the carriage starting to pull away.

"Hold!" Edward cried, chasing after the carriage on foot a good distance before the futility of the action struck him and he returned somewhat sheepishly to Jane.

"Fanny and her betrothed are careful planners," Jane said. "I see they thought of everything."

"Fanny and Lord Grandville? It was she who told me you'd been abducted!" Edward exclaimed, and then grinned as the light dawned.

"Yes," Jane corroborated, and was suddenly overcome with anger and mortification. "How could they! I told her not to interfere in my life. They have left us stranded with one horse, with night coming on and too far away to find shelter. I could strangle them both."

Suddenly Edward tossed back his head and laughed. "Tell me, was Grandville dressed like a highwayman?"

Jane nodded. "It is *not* amusing," she said as Edward laughed harder.

"I think," he said, trying to stop laughing as he put an arm about Jane, "that after they have gone to all this trouble, the least we can do is to get married. I'd rather like to be connected to Fanny and Grandville. Why," he said, pointing to a basket by the side of the road, "he even had them leave us provisions of some sort."

When Jane made no reply, he turned her face to his. "You really have no choice, Jane. We shall be alone together tonight, at an inn if not in the forest. We are too far away from Staplefield or any other town I know of to find proper accommodation, and my horse is too tired to press."

Jane looked into his hazel eyes, and her resistance began to crumble. Her shoulder felt tinglingly aware of his arm and his finger was slowly caressing her cheek, making her breathing short and shallow.

Edward noticed it, too, and bent to kiss her, a kiss that soon became passionate and demanding.

Jane was losing sense of where she was when a nudge on her shoulder caused her to jump. Edward jumped, as well, and laughed when he saw his horse, who had come to remind them he was also there.

"It's lucky we aren't walking," Edward said, taking the reins and helping Jane up on his horse's back.

"If it had been Ariel, no doubt we would be," Jane said, laughing. "He is much too independent to wait patiently for his rider."

Edward went to get the basket that had been left for them and tied it securely on the horse. He swung up behind Jane and they began going slowly down the road.

Jane remembered Lord Blackwood's words and, throwing away the last of her reservations, leaned back onto Edward's chest. His arms tightened about her and he kissed her softly. The motion of the horse and the warmth of Edward's body against hers began to make Jane sleepy.

"Do you think you can believe in my love at last, my English rose?" Edward asked gently.

"Yes, but Jane is from the French," she reminded him sleepily.

You'll flip . . . your pages won't!
Read paperbacks *hands-free* with

Book Mate • I

The perfect "mate" for all your romance paperbacks

Traveling • Vacationing • At Work • In Bed • Studying • Cooking • Eating

Perfect size for all standard paperbacks, this wonderful invention makes reading a pure pleasure! Ingenious design holds paperback books OPEN and FLAT so even wind can't ruffle pages – leaves your hands free to do other things. Reinforced, wipe-clean vinyl-covered holder flexes to let you turn pages without undoing the strap . . . supports paperbacks so well, they have the strength of hardcovers!

Pages turn WITHOUT opening the strap

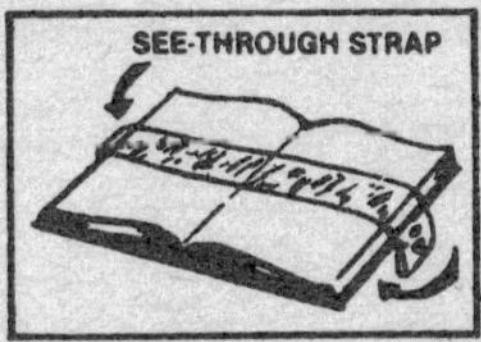

Reinforced back stays flat.

Built in bookmark

10" x 7¼" opened.
Snaps closed for easy carrying, too

Available now. Send your name, address, and zip code, along with a check or money order for just $5.95 + 75¢ for delivery (for a total of $6.70) payable to Reader Service to:

Reader Service
Bookmate Offer
3010 Walden Avenue
P.O. Box 1396
Buffalo, N.Y. 14269-1396

Offer not available in Canada
*New York residents add appropriate sales tax.

BM-GR